DANGEROUS CURVES

BY
KAREN ANDERS

MILLS & BOON

First published in Great Britain 2011
by Mills & Boon, an imprint of Harlequin (UK) Limited,
Eton House, 18-24 Paradise Road, Richmond, Surrey TW9 1SR

© Karen Anders 2008

ISBN: 978 0 263 88065 6

14-0511

Harlequin (UK) policy is to use papers that are natural, renewable and recyclable products and made from wood grown in sustainable forests. The logging and manufacturing processes conform to the legal environmental regulations of the country of origin.

Printed and bound in Spain
by Blackprint CPI, Barcelona

To my critique partners Sarra Maria Cannon and
Jennifer Harrington for reading so much material in
such a short period of time.
I am eternally grateful.

Karen Anders is a three time National Readers' Choice
Award finalist, *Romantic Times* Reviewers Choice
finalist and has won the prestigious HOLT Medallion.
Two of her novels made bestseller lists in 2003. Published
since 1997, she currently writes sexy action/adventure
romance for the Blaze® line. To contact the author please
write to her in care of Harlequin Books, 225 Duncan
Mill Road, Don Mills, Ontario M3B 3K9, or visit www.
karenanders.com.

Dear Reader,

Dangerous curves are hard to maneuver most often because one can't see what is coming around the bend. And as in any dangerous situation, the survivors always rise to the occasion.

That's what happens to Max and Rio. There are many people with hidden agendas and top-secret secrets that must be kept, but what happens when the unexpected occurs and two people fall in love amidst the chaos? When this couple puts their hearts on the line, it's the most tempting danger of all.

Happy reading,

Karen Anders

1

Red.

Sweater.

Short.

Plaid.

Schoolgirl.

Skirt.

Dangerous.

Curves.

The woman was the first thing Special Agent Max Carpenter noticed when he powered into the FBI conference room breathing fire.

The sight of her reversed his own burning anger on himself like a backdraft.

She stood by the window that overlooked downtown Los Angeles illuminated by the light that caught the highlights in her mahogany hair, intensifying every fiery strand.

Cut in layers around her face, it fell in long waves across her shoulders and down to the middle of her back. Her almond eyes, a striking amber color that swirled with remembered pain, peered at him. Her face had a wild, out-there beauty and the cuts and bruises on

her face and arms did nothing to detract from her love-
liness. As soon as he saw the injuries she'd suffered, he
went all tight inside, his fists clenching.

Had the Ghost done this to her?

He could see the abuse she'd suffered in the smudges
beneath her eyes and the pinch in her full, soft-looking lips.

One of her graceful hands was wrapped around her
rib cage as if to support her torso. The other was braced
against the frame of the window.

Large enough to hold twenty people, the room served
as a gathering place for staff meetings and high-level
conferences. The elegance of the room always surprised
him. Comfortable black chairs lined up like soldiers
around the long, polished maple table. A credenza with
a water pitcher and glasses stood at one end of the room
and a state-of-the-art wide-screen monitor and projec-
tor at the other.

The only other man in the room was someone Max
recognized as the director of the DEA, Russell Sanford.
What could the DEA director want with him and what
did it have to do with this woman?

In the world fight against terror, it was now common
for the DEA and FBI to work closely together on
matters that affected national security, so interagency
collaboration wasn't a new concept to Max. The timing
was bad because he was so close to a breakthrough on
the Ghost, a notorious arms dealer and number one on
the FBI's Ten Most Wanted List. But for Max, appre-
hending the Ghost was personal. The Ghost had recently put his sister, Allie Carpenter, in mortal danger
and now her twin, Callie, intended to go undercover to

bring him to justice. Callie worked for a top secret branch of Homeland Security called Watchdog.

Max wasn't willing to take the chance his completely competent sister wouldn't become another victim of the Ghost.

Max's supervisor, Michael Drake, had escorted him to the conference room and now stood near the door like a sentinel. Whatever the director wanted, Max was sure Michael was here to guarantee Max agreed. In fact, Michael had *ordered* him to the meeting when Max was hell-bent on following up on the last lead he'd had for the Ghost.

"Agent Carpenter, I'm Russell Sanford, Director of the DEA."

"A pleasure to meet you, sir," Max replied. He kept the woman in his sight, not only because his awareness of her was like a buzz in his brain, trailing down his spine like the whine of a chain saw set on high, but also because she looked like a stiff wind could blow her away at any minute.

"I want you to protect one of my best agents, Rio Marshall."

Max turned toward her again. This delicate, stunning woman was a DEA agent? She was about one hundred and ten pounds soaking wet. He couldn't imagine her elegant hand wrapped around a Glock, let alone taking down a man with her bare hands. But he could imagine her hand wrapped around him. Those soft hands could cause a lot of friction moving over his flesh. Bad thoughts. Bad, bad thoughts.

She focused on him, but almost as an afterthought. She didn't want to be here any more than he did.

"With all due respect, sir, why the FBI?"

"We believe there's a mole in the DEA and we don't want to take the risk that whoever is leaking information will give away Agent Marshall's position. She's still recovering from her injuries and is at risk."

The woman snorted but said nothing.

"Why me?" Max asked, breaking the suddenly tense silence.

"You come recommended."

Max just didn't buy it. There were agents at the bureau who had more experience and others who would be better suited as a bodyguard. And why was the DEA director here instead of her division boss? The chain of command had been breached, but Max didn't know why. He kept his questions to himself, well aware he could jeopardize his job if he decided to rock the boat just a little bit more.

"What happened?" Max addressed the question to Rio, but she turned toward the window.

Sanford answered for her. "She was on a mission in Colombia and it went down bad. We rescued her last week. Unfortunately, her memory is sketchy regarding the incident, but she remembers seeing the Ghost. At this time, she can't recall any details of his face, but in time we're hoping she regains her memory."

At first Max had been totally against babysitting, but now he realized who she was and what the Ghost had done to her, he couldn't say no to protecting her from harm. The information she had locked in her head would be valuable in tracking down and eliminating the Ghost once and for all. The Ghost would cease to be a threat to Callie and Max would get justice for what he'd put Allie through.

"What is the plan?"

"We booked you into a private hotel for the next two weeks," Sanford said.

"In L.A.?" Max asked.

"No, Hawaii. We'd like you off the radar and out of California altogether."

"So you think the Ghost will try to kill her?"

"Yes, we do. No one's ever seen his face. He's taken great pains to keep his identity a secret. We know he's courting Eduardo Fuentes and Agent Marshall was just recently a prisoner of Fuentes's," Sanford said, pouring himself a glass of water and taking a sip.

Max stared at Sanford and let that bit of 411, with all its implications, sink in to his suspicious mind.

"Two weeks?" Max said. A private hotel, for cripes sake. An island retreat with Rio Marshall? What would be the hard part?

Oh, yeah, keeping her alive and keeping his hands off her.

Sanford nodded. He glanced at Max's supervisor, then at Rio. She stared impassively back and still said nothing.

His hyperawareness of her climbed a notch every time he looked at her. He shifted his shoulders and rested against the conference table.

"We should have everything wrapped up by then and it should be safe for her to return."

"Wrapped up?" Max repeated.

"A car is scheduled to pick you up in fifteen minutes."

"I haven't packed…." Max found it interesting Sanford had no intention of telling him what would be *wrapped* up.

"You can get what you need in Maui. Agent Marshall has what she needs. Isn't that correct, Agent Marshall?"

"Yes, sir," she answered, emphasizing the "sir," her lush mouth pulling into a sullen grimace.

The sound of her husky voice was like embers from a fire. Embers that burned inside and out. Damn. Not convenient. He was supposed to protect her…and not from himself.

"Thank you for your dedicated service, Agent Carpenter." The DEA Director shook hands with Max and then his boss. He left the room.

"Why don't you make yourself comfortable and I'll have my assistant let you know when the car is here," Max's supervisor said.

Max nodded and his supervisor left, closing the door behind him.

Once Sanford had left the room, and the conference door closed, Rio doubled over like a puppet whose strings had been severed. She gasped softly, her face going a shade paler, if that was possible. Max reached her side in seconds and steadied her as she teetered.

Wrapping his arm around her, he held her so she could get her bearings. Splaying one of her hands on his chest, her palm warm against his dress shirt, she closed her fingers around the material as if to anchor herself. His altruistic urge got blindsided by the attraction he found he couldn't shake, even as he realized she was injured more than she was letting on.

He held her tightly, but gently. When her eyes met his, they captured him like a net and for a moment the world faded and it was only the two of them, him giving her what she needed and her giving acceptance.

In his attempt to support her, his thigh slipped between her legs and for a moment she rode him, her sexy skirt bunching and revealing more of her creamy thigh…and more bruises.

Emotions tumbled through him. Anger that she'd been so mistreated, protectiveness and the need to soothe her, kiss away the pain she must have endured. The force of the emotions startled him and he pivoted on his heel and measured how far it was to one of the conference chairs.

"I'm okay," she said softly as if it hurt her to breathe.

"Like hell you are. You don't have to pretend for me, Agent Marshall."

She clutched at her ribs. "You don't have to *Agent* me, Max. Just call me Rio." Her voice sounded compressed, as if she were forcing words out of her throat.

"Broken ribs?"

"Just bruised."

"Hurts though?"

"Like a son of a gun," she said with a brief smile.

"I get it. You didn't want to look weak in front of the DEA Director."

"It shouldn't matter that I look like a delicate little flower. I can hold my own and have on many occasions."

Grit. He liked that.

He watched her close her eyes and try to breathe around the pain. When she opened them, for a moment, he was lost.

Damn she was beautiful. He couldn't help but stare as her words washed over him like air currents.

"Your supervisors ever heard of steel magnolias? There are plenty of men, especially bad men, who don't think much of women and underestimate them all the time. A plus for us," Max said.

"The powers that be at the DEA say I'm better suited using my womanly wiles undercover rather than brute force."

She had the kind of hair that made a man want to run his hands through it to see how silky it was. It accentuated her fine, high cheekbones.

And that mouth. Lush, full lips made for a man to kiss. Plump and inviting.

"Like I'm some kind of Mata Hari."

"You've got the looks for it."

"My skills are just as deadly as yours, Max. Make no mistake about that. It galls me to have to admit I need help."

"It's not weak to admit it, Rio. Maybe you should sit down. I'll get you some water."

"Okay."

PLEASE DON'T LET HIM be nice, Rio thought as he walked over to the credenza and poured water from a pitcher.

She'd felt poleaxed when he'd walked into the room. Tall, dark and handsome had nothing on him. Those broad shoulders, tapering down to his trim waist, didn't help. The blue of his suit brought out the blue of his eyes and his dark, curly hair only accentuated those eyes all the more.

When he made eye contact, she sighed. There was

something in those killer baby blues, something so open, so easy, so…so…compassionate. As if he cared about her without really knowing her.

What she had to do would be hard enough without having to like the guy, too.

He brought the water over and flashed her a smile. She reached for the glass and their hands touched. For a moment, he stared at her.

Like taking candy from a baby. She'd always had the ability to make men swoon, and even though her step-brother had cautioned her on using her beauty to get what she wanted, she found herself using it constantly in her job.

She'd seduced many a criminal with only her charms and gotten plenty of them to give her exactly what she needed to fulfill her mission. Bringing them to justice had given her a lot of satisfaction.

Unfortunately, this *assignment* they'd given her wasn't going to give her any satisfaction at all.

They had been desperate. The director played on her loyalties to the agency. Max Carpenter was a wild card and could disrupt a very delicate, top secret mission, as well as endanger a key undercover DEA agent who was currently working in the field. She hadn't been privy to the mission particulars. All she knew was that the mission had something to do with the Ghost and the director wanted Max out of the picture.

Rio knew all about Max's family and how just recently Allie Carpenter had saved a very important undercover operation. Allie's twin sister, Callie, worked for Watchdog, an agency that brought illegal gunrunners to justice. When Allie was posing as her undercover persona, Gina Callahan, to snag the Ghost, a rival gunrunner tried to kill her and put her out of commission. Without Allie spearheading the deal, the whole sting would have been a wash. Watchdog recruited Callie to step in to cover for the hospitalized Allie. Drew Miller had trained Allie for the mission and that's how they met. Drew Miller had been the agent who had saved Rio from Fuentes's compound.

So Max had the same motivation as Rio. Rio wanted to get justice for her stepbrother, Shane, and Max wanted revenge on the Ghost for putting both his sisters in danger.

She had told her boss that it would just be easier to fire him rather than go through all these machinations, but her boss said that short of jailing Max, it wouldn't have stopped him from his pursuit of the Ghost. The matter for Max was more personal. Rather than lose Max as an agent, they just needed him distracted for a short period of time until the mission was over.

Now that she'd met him, she could understand why Max's supervisor and the director were so worried. Max struck her as the kind of man who did not give up on what he believed. He was tenacious, principled and noble all wrapped up in a lethal, intelligent package.

Duping the really sharp, drop-dead-gorgeous special agent wasn't going to be a cakewalk.

She'd earn brownie points, though. She'd need them. She'd screwed up in Colombia. She'd screwed up bad. She wouldn't rest until the man who'd killed her stepbrother was brought to justice. Eduardo Fuentes had to pay.

She had every intention of going back to Colombia

and getting a better look. That man she'd seen with Fuentes…there was something very familiar about him and she hadn't been able to stop thinking about his shadowed profile.

The water soothed her parched throat and she felt a tiny bit guilty she'd overplayed her injuries. She found a lot of men in law enforcement were very protective and a swooning woman hit all the right buttons. She couldn't say she wouldn't want to hit some of his other buttons. Being cradled in his arms made her forget about the bruised ribs that were all too real.

She downplayed her experience in her head because it was so much easier than dealing with what had happened to her at the hands of Eduardo Fuentes. She knew her stepbrother would never have backed down from a challenge, and she had no intention of backing down, either.

"Better?" he asked.

She nodded and gave him a smile. His eyes lit up and he smiled back. Whoa, he was a loaded weapon and deadly with that smile.

"So, I'm sorry to pull you off whatever case you were working on to babysit me. I really don't need a bodyguard. Too bad they're worried about a mole. Looks like we have to play in the same sandbox for a little while."

"I don't mind kicking up some sand, Rio, as long as we're honest with each other. Misinformation can be a dangerous thing."

Rio bit her lip. She was already getting herself in trouble here. She absolutely hated this assignment, but the thought of an agent, someone like her stepbrother, losing his life due to interference in an investigation was more than her conscience could bear. She only had to keep him busy for two weeks, and then she'd be healed and ready to go at Fuentes again.

She smiled and nodded. "We have an interagency agreement." She hoped this all wouldn't backfire on her.

The door opened and the supervisor's assistant let them know the car was downstairs.

Max put out his hand to help her up. Rio hesitated slightly before she slid her palm over his, trying to tamp down the excitement the warmth of his hand generated deep in the pit of her stomach.

A tropical paradise—warm sands, ocean breezes and decadence were almost enough to send her into another swoon, but add sexy Max Carpenter to that mix and it almost seemed, well…criminal.

TURNED ON AT 30,000 FEET. Probably made him a candidate for the Mile High Club, but engaging in sex in a tiny bathroom didn't appeal to Max. He liked space and time to indulge himself in a woman, steep himself in her scent and the softness of her skin, take his sweet time in making her come long and hard.

The DEA hadn't skimped on their accommodations. They were seated in first class with all the amenities—fancy booze, gourmet food and comfortable, spacious seats. But at this moment Max was crowded. Rio Marshall had fallen asleep shortly after takeoff. Her head had landed on his shoulder as soon as the "buckle seat belt" sign clicked off, and was now nestled against him, her copper hair spread all over his suit jacket.

When the flight attendant passed him, Max stopped her. "Could I get a blanket for the lady?"

"Certainly, sir," the attendant said and she returned quickly with a blanket. He covered Rio, that damn protective instinct kicking in again. He couldn't seem to help it. She may need his protection for the short term, but she was a seasoned agent and he was sure she had considerable skills. But she looked so defenseless with her dusky lashes against her pale cheeks. He could see more bruises she'd attempted to cover with makeup and he got angry all over again.

He loosened his tie and then pulled it off, unbuttoning a couple of his shirt buttons to get more comfortable.

Their flight was an hour to Honolulu and then another forty minutes to Maui.

Rio shifted in her sleep with a small moan that sliced through him with unexpected desire. The soft noise mimicked what she would sound like in the throes of passion. Her hand slid up his torso and rested at the base of his throat, her palm hot against his skin. The blanket slipped and exposed her long, shapely legs. Her delicate feet were wrapped in strappy sandals and her toenails painted a deep, passionate red.

He got hard just sitting here with her warm, pliant body against his, her soft hair tickling his chin, as he took in her clean, female scent every time he inhaled.

She moaned again, her eyes fluttering, but this time she was in distress. She shifted again and whimpered, her breathing coming faster.

"Rio," he said softly, touching her shoulder. She jerked awake, her eyes open wide and frightened. "It's okay." He soothed her. "We're on a plane on our way to Hawaii. You're okay."

With a soft cry she buried her face in his neck, her whole body trembling. Max gathered her close, holding her instinctively, knowing she needed the closeness and the comfort after her nightmare that was all too real.

His hand came up to smooth through her hair, and it was softer than it looked as he cradled her head.

"Man that was bad. I dreamed about my stepbrother and a day at the beach that turned bad. That's odd."

"Going through what you went through with the Ghost could mess with your head. Did you talk to your shrink?"

She raised her head, a wry look on her face. "Yes, I talked to her and she helped. But it was only four days ago and I just got out of the hospital."

"Who got you out of Colombia?"

"A guy named Drew Miller and his team. They literally blew up part of Fuentes's compound to get me out. I guess they wanted me back."

"Miller? He's going to be my new brother-in-law. He's engaged to my sister Allie."

"No kidding."

She seemed to realize she was plastered to him and she moved away, suddenly self-conscious. Max would have been content to hold her all the way to Honolulu. His gut said there was something "off" about her he couldn't quite put his finger on. She seemed so strong, but then…he wasn't sure how to read her.

"Excuse me," Rio said as she rose. "I need to use the bathroom."

Max rose, too, and Rio squeezed by him, so close her breasts brushed against his chest.

He couldn't help but watch as she made her way unsteadily down the aisle.

When he realized he was staring, he directed his attention away and sat down. But within minutes he felt a tap on his shoulder. Rio stood at his elbow. "I…ah…need your help."

"Sure. What is it?"

"My bandage from my ribs has loosened and I just can't get it tight enough. It's at least bearable when it's tight, but when it's loose…"

He rose. "I guess the bathroom would be the best place."

"Yes. I'm really sorry for bothering you."

"It's no bother." Max's eyes followed her curvy body down the aisle. She slipped inside the bathroom and he followed her in.

"I know this is awkward, but I have to lift your sweater."

"Sure."

He put his hands on her waist and rolled the sweater up all the way to her lacy, bright red, sexy bra, the soft skin of her torso smooth and warm beneath his hands.

He released the clips on her bandage and unwound it from around her ribs. Then he swore loud and long.

"What is it?"

He inhaled and closed his eyes at the damage they'd done to her. "Bastards. I'd like to get my hands on them."

She looked down and realization dawned on her face. "Oh, the bruises. Yeah, they look pretty bad."

"Pretty bad? They were brutal."

"They wanted to know who I was and why I was there. When I didn't give them any information, it made them really mad. They worked me over and threw me in a cell. I'm sure there would have been worse treatment, but Drew Miller showed up and got me out. I don't remember much after that."

"How tight do you want it?"

"Snug, but not too tight."

He started to wrap the bandage and tried to be gentle, but she gasped. "I'm sorry."

"It's not your fault. It's just really sore."

"How's that?"

"That's good."

He secured the bandage. But before he could pull down her sweater, the plane jerked and she was thrown against him. As his back hit the door, his arms went around her to keep her ribs from taking any more damage. Her body was tight against his from his chest to his groin, her sweet face and lush lips inches from his own.

She stared up at him, her features softening. "Thank you for saving my ribs. You are my hero."

He smiled slightly because she was trying to be funny in a funny situation, but her humor only added to his attraction to her.

Her eyes were deep and dark, guarding her secrets in that enigmatic way that only women possessed.

He'd experienced pure chemistry before, but with this woman, it was so much more than that. He wanted to get into her head, into her body and into her heart. His head descended, his mouth covered hers.

He kissed her with hunger and unadulterated need. His tongue dove deep, seeking the intimate flavor beyond her lips. His hands went to her butt, gripping her bottom tight, and dragged her into him, forcing her legs to widen against his hips so the thick length of his cock pressed hard, insistent and intimate against her damp heat.

She slid her arms around his neck and wrapped one of her long, slender legs around his leg. He leaned more fully into her and instinctively thrust, straining to get closer, just as she arched rhythmically against him in perfect unison. Had it not been for her insubstantial panties and the material of his dress pants separating them, the motion would have caused him to slide deep inside her…right where he wanted to be.

He groaned at the incredible surge of hot, carnal lust that kicked up his adrenaline a few notches. He felt primal and possessive and ravenous, burning up from the inside out and unable to get enough of this woman who affected him not only sexually, but also on a deeper level he'd yet to fully define. All he knew was he had to have her, and then he'd work on unraveling the mystery surrounding her, the contradictions, and the secrets she seemed determined to keep. He already knew one night with her wasn't going to be enough for him.

She moaned and panted against his lips, her thigh locking along the back of his thigh as her hips rocked and gyrated against his shaft. He felt her shudder and was stunned to realize she was on the precarious verge of coming…just like this. She seemed to realize it at the same moment, too, and with a soft gasp she pressed her palms against his shoulders in an attempt to push him away and stop the spiraling madness.

But he wasn't about to let such a provocative encounter end without giving her the release her body so obviously needed. Wrenching his mouth from hers, he stared into her bright, startled eyes, all the while keeping up the steady pressure and the illicit friction that was driving her toward that ultimate peak of pleasure.

He saw her fear and the pain she'd endured and he saw the need for her to experience *life* after coming so close to death. "Let it happen. Take what you need," he said.

His words must have struck a chord with her, because she did exactly that. Her hands relaxed and slid down his chest, and she tossed her head back with a soft, dissolving kind of moan. Her body arched into his one last time before she succumbed to the orgasm she'd been desperately trying to hold at bay.

Muscles wired taut with discipline, he gritted his teeth to keep from tumbling over the same edge that promised pure ecstasy. Instead he focused on her beautiful face as she came, captivated by her sensuality and enthralled by her candid response.

A sigh of contentment escaped her lips and she drifted back in slow, gradual degrees, her half-mast eyes a languid shade of amber. She looked incredibly sexy and fulfilled.

He couldn't help himself. Everything about Rio Marshall was gunslinger-tough, even her name. It wasn't anything overt she was doing, just the entire package she presented.

He hadn't meant to kiss her, but her silky voice and her soft body—along with the courage it must have taken to defy her captors—and the abuse she'd suffered were all too much.

He'd always been drawn to strength. Something she had in spades.

Rio looked up at him as dazed as he was. "This is very inconvenient, Agent Carpenter."

He'd faced danger head-on, sudden danger, and known danger, but kissing Rio and making her come were two of the most dangerous acts he'd ever performed. She was supposed to be a job.

But now he wanted a lot more than to protect her with his body—he wanted her body under him, on top of him, all over him.

Max felt a settling deep inside where he was always restless. Something was changing inside him and he was powerless to stop it.

All of a sudden, sex in an airplane bathroom didn't seem like such a bad idea.

2

"HEY, ARE YOU almost done in there? There's a line out here."

Rio's eyes snapped open and she pushed away from his chest. Well, she could check one thing off her clandestine list. She'd seduced Max Carpenter, except he'd turned the tables on her and he'd been the one doing all the work and she'd reaped the rewards.

She could tell by the look in his eyes the people outside the door didn't bother him and the part of her that lived for the adrenaline rush wanted to forget about them, too. But she must not be too wanton, too eager, and give up the prize too soon.

It didn't help that Max was one of the good guys. And considering he was also the epitome of a bad boy was quite an intoxicating mix. And doubly dangerous. To her, and to her mission. From the moment she'd met Max, she had this uncontrollable urge to confide in him. And, just now, she wanted to lean on him, wanted things she couldn't have. But for Rio that was out of the question. She'd been making her own way since her stepbrother, Shane, had given his life in the war against drugs.

She pushed away from him, fighting an internal battle of want over necessity. This man made it easy to play the siren. One look from him and she felt like some primal creature whose only edict was to dissolve him down to his most fundamental core. It was a wonder they both hadn't gone up in flames. And God help her, it was her mission to do so. In her mind, keeping him occupied hadn't really involved anything physical between them. Rio could have avoided it and still kept him right where she wanted him. But that was before she'd met him.

"The move is yours," Max said.

"This isn't some chess game. There are angry people out there who need to take care of a different bodily function. They get just as testy about their needs as we do."

"I doubt that, but I'm trained to handle them."

"I bet you can handle just about anything."

He laughed. "That was before I met you."

"We're supposed to be focusing on hiding. Inciting an angry mob on an airplane is a good way to draw attention to ourselves. This is supposed to be about business," Rio said.

"FBI and DEA business," he said.

Rio got a glimpse of that slick, intelligent mind. "Bodyguard business," she corrected.

"I'm thinking about your body right now." His grin was as unabashed as ever. He pressed his hips against hers, making them both groan just a little.

"I can see and, oh, my, feel you are, but let's let these people get on with their…business."

Some of the fog blessedly lifted from his eyes. "Okay, Rio, but I've got a feeling you can handle yourself quite easily without a bodyguard."

"Except I'm injured."

"True," he said.

She disengaged her hands from his and tried to put some distance between them. She hadn't expected to feel such a strong tug. A tug that wasn't entirely physical. It was bad enough he could make her body tremble in need with nothing more than a glance and a smile. Her heart absolutely could not—would not—come into play. And yet she was looking at him and feeling something was undeniably out of control.

Foolhardy indeed.

She needed to get some distance from him, and quickly, if she was going to think even a bit clearly on the matter. For whatever reason—and she was certain he had one—he let her go.

She thought she'd been having a crappy day when she'd so badly bungled her one prime opportunity to get some dirt on Eduardo Fuentes. Now, she was away from Colombia and her one objective, completing a mission she didn't want to complete. Duping a man like Max would come back to haunt her. She knew it.

But a DEA agent's life hung in the balance and Max's investigation could put that agent's life in danger.

When she was ready to leave, Max opened the door. He stepped out and held out his hand. Rio took it, the warmth of his palm like a shock to her system. She held her ribs as she stepped over the threshold, making it clear to the people waiting she was injured. Some eyes were sly, but she ignored them as she followed him back to their seats.

"That was decidedly embarrassing."

"Ha. All those guys wish they could step out of an airplane lavatory with a woman like you with your beautiful face and all this amazing red hair."

He said it easily, without artifice.

A blush stained her cheeks, catching her off guard. It was surprising she had this reaction now, as what they had done together in the lavatory made blushing seem ridiculous.

It was true their interactions had been lustful, but the fact he had said something so earnest, and so…genuine made her react in ways that were dangerous to say the least. Such as wondering what it would be like to be with Max in regular, day-to-day situations, where she wouldn't have to watch every word, every move she made, looking for potential danger to her mission. It was a jarring concept.

She slid into her seat. "Thank you for the compliment," she said, still struggling to reset her equilibrium even now that his hands weren't on her. "But we need to remember why we're on this plane and heading out of Los Angeles."

"The Ghost," Max growled. "I was getting close. I could feel it."

"It sounds personal."

"It is. And it's professional, too. And how about you? What got you into hot water in Colombia? Sounds like you made a bad decision, or worse, one that didn't involve intellect, but emotion."

She was silent for a moment, and then said, "Touché, Max." Her personal agenda regarding her stepbrother was her business. She didn't share with people and she certainly wasn't going to share with Max. She tightened her resolve. She only had to distract Max for two weeks. Then she would be healed and ready to tackle Fuentes again.

"What were you after there?" Max asked.

"I was on a mission."

"For the DEA?" Max shifted his broad shoulders so he was turned toward her.

"I can't divulge any information about why I was there," Rio said, crossing her legs and looking away from his bright blue eyes. She had no intention of getting into this type of discussion with Max. *Keep It Simple, Stupid* was her motto.

"Evasive answers, but I didn't expect any less from a field agent."

"And your pursuit of the Ghost. Is that sanctioned?" Rio opened up her packet of peanuts and popped one into her mouth.

"You are aware I can't divulge any information about an open case."

"Good answer," she said. "But I didn't expect any less from a field agent."

He smiled then, and it wasn't any less powerful this time around than it had been in the lavatory. His entire aura changed when he did that. He looked like a trouble-maker and those types always dragged the unsuspecting into their shenanigans.

"I guess we know where we stand here."

"I guess we do," she agreed. He was already sorely testing her sense of balance. Their chance bond was as unexpected as it was unwanted. At least on her end. She didn't mind him being more approachable, but she could ill afford to let herself become more attracted to him. Letting anyone get close right now would be a major risk. Besides, her time here was limited, so what was the point? All she had to do was resist temptation. Very potent temptation.

Putting the mission at the forefront of her mind, she worked to keep the conversation teasing, but controlled. "If you were going to Hawaii on vacation, what would you do?"

"Windsurf, surf and snorkel."

"Water sports. Did you spend a lot of time at the beach?"

He laughed, and she had to note his charm was much more lethal when he was amused. "I wish. I come from a small town you've probably never heard of—Covina."

"I know that city. It's just outside L.A. and isn't connected to the freeway. So that would mean you were landlocked. Bummer."

"How did you know that?"

"Big fan of Joan Jett. She went to high school there."

"I wouldn't have pegged you for a hard-rocking babe."

"I was, to the detriment of my parents. Shane didn't help. He bought me her CDs."

"Where is your family now?" Max asked.

"Gone. Car accident, almost four years ago now, during a trip to Monterey. Bad brakes."

"I'm very sorry," he said, quite sincerely. For all his dark intensity, he had a very warm, soothing tone to his voice. It made a person want to lean closer.

She nodded and shifted away. It was an easier physical shift than the mental one she really needed to make. "Thank you. I am, too. I miss them very much." She put on a smile.

Thankfully, he didn't press any further. It was going to be difficult enough being around him and keeping her guard up. The less they shared the better. It was just…a lot harder than she'd expected it would be. In less than a few hours, he'd already learned more about her than the people she worked next to all day, and had for the time she'd been in the DEA.

She looked out the window just as the captain came on the intercom and hit the seat-belt sign. They were coming in for a landing in Maui.

Let the games begin.

THE DEA HAD GOTTEN THEM a suite located at the end of the hotel with close exits. Clothes were already hung in the closet for both of them.

Rio merely glanced at the standard two queen beds in the room. But the sight of the two beds disappointed her.

"You gotta love the DEA. They're as good as Triple A."

Max chuckled as he looked over the clothing, nodding at what he found. "Shorts and loud shirts. What else?"

Rio picked up the backpack she'd ordered and immediately started stuffing it with essentials.

"What are you doing?"

"I always have a flee bag in case I have to run."

"I'm sure that comes in handy in some of the situations you've been in."

"It has and has saved my life quite a few times. I'm going to change into a suit and go sit on the beach. I need to soak up some sun."

He shrugged. "Sounds good. Are you hungry?"

She turned toward him. There was hunger there and it was all hot and heavy in his eyes. *Hungry* was an understatement.

She rolled her eyes. "No, not right now." But his smile was one of pure fun and mischief, and she wished like hell it didn't make her want to be just as mischievous in return. Wouldn't it shock him if she sauntered over to the bed and simply took him down to the mattress for the next few hours? The images that immediately played through her now-feverish mind made her turn firmly toward the closet instead. She skimmed over the array of clothing hanging in front of her and had to give it to the DEA personnel who'd done the shopping. Everything she needed was there. She pulled out a sexy red bikini and rolled her eyes. Could they have been any more blatant? She headed to the bathroom to change. She did manage to pull herself together enough to pause before stepping inside.

She looked back at him. "I had a snack on the plane and it's filled me right up."

"Sure you don't need help with the ribs?"

She smiled. "No, it's nice and snug. You did *such* a *good* job in the airplane lavatory."

He sighed and his eyes never left her until she closed the door.

She didn't know whether to laugh or bang her head against the wall. If she thought it would knock some sense into her, she would have started banging away. But that amused and tempting look on his face only made her laugh.

"I learn fast."

She jumped. His voice was close and only flimsy wood separated them.

"I wouldn't expect anything less of a field agent."

His laugh was rich, and deep, and so incredibly sexy she closed her eyes to keep from jerking the door open and having her way with him. She removed the pressure bandage around her ribs and breathed deeply. Okay, still a little sore, but not bad. The bruises weren't pretty, but they'd begun to fade. She quickly pulled on the red bikini and the white eyelet cover-up. Now this was an outfit that would entice him. The eyelet framed her generous breasts and the hem came down to the tops of her thighs.

She slipped her feet into a pair of black flip-flops, and then looked in the mirror. She looked pale and drawn. Sun would really help to revitalize her. She couldn't remember the last time she'd had a vacation. Consumed with her job of bringing down Fuentes, she'd neglected to take time to renew and regenerate. Well, these two weeks would serve as her vacation. She was in Hawaii with a delicious and delectable man. So, she had to give up a little bit of herself for the job. It would be easy with Max.

Her first instinct was to stay where she was to avoid the pull of him, but that would be detrimental to her mission. So, instead of remaining out of his line of sight and out of his reach, she approached him and let him get a load of her outfit. She even went so far as to run her fingers down the swell of her breasts to draw his eyes right where she wanted them. Distract and conquer. Male hormones were her ally here.

"Nice view," he said.

"As I said, the DEA is as good as Triple A. There's nothing like the ocean," she said, turning to him and running her hand through her hair.

Her little strategy with the eyelet worked to perfection. When he glanced over his shoulder, he did a double take that heated her body and tingled her senses. This was going to be a problem if she couldn't separate her own desire from this seduction. She'd have to work harder at that.

"Yeah, I'll say." He was making it clear that he was referring not to the view below, but to the one standing in front of him. It was like taking candy from a baby. Still, Max was a mission and nothing more, despite the fact that her body definitely wanted *more*.

"So, I guess we should begin Mission Laze About."

"Lead the way."

Making sure they had their key cards, they exited the room and headed down to the lobby. They proceeded to the back of the hotel and the brightly colored cabana chairs located at the pool and on the sand, affording the lounger a glorious view of the sea-green ocean.

Out of habit, as they approached the lobby, Rio did a quick scan. A man was trying to settle down a rambunctious child, a woman was using a tiny compact to put on her lipstick and a burly man walked away from the front desk toward the elevator. A sense of danger coiled within her. Did she know this guy from one of her missions? Her brain was fuzzy.

"What's wrong?" Max asked.

"I think I recognized someone, but I can't place where." She felt annoyed and awkward with the information inside her head that wasn't accessible. The damn drugs they gave her, along with the conk on the head, made her second-guess herself. She hated second-guessing herself.

"Want me to check it out?"

"No, he never even looked in this direction. I'm sure it's nothing, just my overactive imagination running away with me."

"Are you sure?"

"Yes, let's go to the beach."

The day was warm and the feel of the sun on her skin made her sigh. She found a beach chair tucked in to a small cove a little ways from the main part of the hotel and sank down into it. Pulling suntan lotion out of her bag, she turned to Max.

"Could you do my back?"

"I'll do anything you want me to, especially when it comes to your body. I'm supposed to be guarding it."

She smiled. "Such a dedicated agent."

He straddled the cabana chair and patted the seat. Rio got comfortable and handed him the lotion. "Rub it in good. I don't want to burn," she said a bit breathlessly as his palms flattened on her back and started to rub and slide upward. Her eyes closed as his big, clever hands moved from the small of her back to her shoulders and then down her arms.

"How's that?" he murmured, his mouth next to her ear. Then he drew his hands down her arms, making her skin tingle at the warm contact.

She had to work to keep still and not arch into his hands as he rubbed. His knuckles barely brushed the swell of her breasts as his hands continued up and down her arms. Her nipples tightened almost painfully, wanting contact that wasn't appropriate even for this sparsely populated beach. The lack of direct stimulation was almost more erotic than if he'd teased and tweaked her.

He moved then and she felt momentarily bereft. But he was soon kneeling in the warm sand and adding more lotion to his hands. "Lift your leg," he ordered.

He massaged his thumbs into the muscles of her legs, digging his fingers in lightly along her inner thigh, before continuing down around her calf. He carefully moved around every bruise, cut and abrasion with gentle ease. When he cupped her foot, she made a soft gasp. Feeling his hands mold every curve of her body, except those that craved his touch most, was far more stimulating than she'd ever imagined. One thing his slow, methodical journey had accomplished was to dismantle her ability to think about anything other than where he was going to touch her next.

It was hard not to be restless, to move her torso, shift her limbs, in an effort to ease the ache that had pervaded her every muscle and pore.

He teased his fingertips along the arch of her foot. A dark brow rose over one of those disarming, see-everything eyes of his as he moved to her other leg and slathered more lotion, using his hands to massage it into her skin. He rose and gently did her face, neck and upper chest, brushing tantalizingly close to the swell of her breasts.

He rubbed his thumb along his hard jaw in an absent caress, studying her from across the expanse of space separating them. "My turn," he said softly and removed his shirt.

Rio stared and for a moment had to pay homage to the muscle gods. He wasn't just muscular. He was honed to a hard, cutting edge. Her fingers itched to touch him. If he'd been a sword, he'd have been a killing blade.

His wide, hard chest tapered down to a taut waist with the definition of those knee-melting oblique muscles fully defined.

When she didn't move, he held out the bottle of lotion. "Come on, you're not afraid of me, are you?"

"Should I be?"

"Depends on the situation and circumstances," he said, giving her the distinct impression he was testing her, though she had no idea why. "Yes or no?"

Her heart beat hard in her chest, the thrill of the forbidden heightening her anticipation. "No, I'm not afraid of you."

"Let's get going before I burn."

Rio was coming to realize Max Carpenter was a take-no-prisoners kind of guy both in the field and in his personal life.

He stood there casually, so utterly male, so intensely

sexual without trying to be, while waiting for her to obey his command. The challenge in his gaze was entirely unapologetic, as if he had every right to be confident. As if he knew she found his calm self-assurance not only a challenge, but a huge turn-on as well.

He was right.

"Now that would be a terrible shame."

She could only imagine what he had in mind for her, but she was ready for anything. Anticipation swirled low in her belly and, unable to resist his allure, she tugged on his wrist and pulled him down onto the cabana chair. She had used her sexuality while in the field, playing a brazen, fearless vixen and a sweet ingenue ripe for a sexual fling, but with Max, she couldn't help being herself.

"Turn around," she demanded and he complied. She squeezed a generous amount of the lotion onto her palms and rubbed them together. Placing her hands on his wide, ripped back, she smoothed in the lotion with circular strokes. He felt deliciously warm and sleek, exceptionally hard in all the right places, and she savored his virile strength as she moved across his broad shoulders. When she switched to the nape of his neck, his silky dark curls tickled the back of her hand, and it was his turn to gasp. That small sound twisted her insides like one of the pretzels they sold on the boardwalk.

Ignoring the twinge in her ribs, she rose and went to face him. "It would be easier if you stood while I do your chest."

"I can take care of my chest just fine," he said, reaching for the lotion in her hand.

"So can I," she said, jerking the bottle away from him. She could lie to herself right now and say this was part of the seduction plan she was weaving around him, but Rio tried to keep herself on the straight and narrow. She wanted to touch him, needed to touch him, had to touch him.

He sighed and spread his hands, but his eyes twinkled. She was once again struck by how incessantly blue they were. It was like staring into an endless sea, sparkling with sunlight. "Have at it, then."

"Ah, you give up way too easily."

"What can I say? I'm easy."

"Ha. I doubt that."

"Then give me the bottle. I say if you want something done right, do it yourself."

"You'd have to get it," she said with a challenge.

He grabbed her around the waist, careful of her ribs, but her laughter gusted out as she switched hands and kept the bottle away, hurting her ribs anyway.

Jockeying for position, he reached for the bottle again, but Rio used her foot to trip him and almost got away. She got tangled up in him and they both fell to the sand, laughing like fools.

Then their eyes met and Rio felt a magnetic pull and for a moment she couldn't breathe. Panic engulfed her, spread through her like wildfire with a warning. Danger. She laughed again and broke eye contact. Standing awkwardly, she handed him the bottle of lotion.

"You win. Here you go."

She was a confident woman who handled her affairs, both private and public, with relative ease. But this man had so totally made her a wanton. All the people who had been close to her were dead. No one had tapped in to her core as he had done, and he'd done so almost effortlessly. A moment ago, she had let down her barriers, actually been herself and not a role she was playing.

She tried her best to appear unaffected and coolly in control as she walked back to her cabana chair and settled into it.

Out of the corner of her eye she could see him still lying in the sand looking at the bottle as if it could give him answers to her switch in mood.

She didn't want him to get to know her more intimately. She'd had enough of relationships that ended badly and this setup would end in two weeks. Keeping things strictly physical was the only way there could be anything between them.

And that sounded like one of the toughest missions she'd ever undertaken in her life.

3

MAX SAT IN THE SAND with the lotion bottle in his hands and asked himself what the hell he was doing. He felt almost as if he'd been released from a spell.

It seemed that ever since he'd met Rio Marshall his focus went by the wayside, and it wasn't like him. Damn hormones.

The truth of the matter was he'd decided to go along with her and see where it took him. If it took him inside Rio, he wouldn't complain.

He rose. Glancing over at her, he saw she'd closed her eyes. Was it meant to shut him out or was she just tired from the flight and the tussle with him? She did look drawn, her skin tone a bit gray.

But the rest of her. Jeez. The rest of her was perfect. His life couldn't possibly be this complicated or this crazy. He should be in his office at the FBI, hot on the trail of the Ghost. He shouldn't have been pulled off his active cases and given this P Triple-A job—Protect Another Agent's Ass. He looked away.

He was all for interdepartmental cooperation, but there were other guys, veteran guys who would have been better suited to babysit Rio Marshall. Max had to ask himself again. Why him?

"You are going to hurt yourself over there," Rio murmured.

He turned to look at her; her eyes were open and staring at him.

"What do you mean?"

"You're thinking really hard. I was afraid your head might explode."

"You don't find this all very strange?" Max asked.

"What?"

"My being chosen to guard you."

Rio shrugged. "Why would I think that was strange? I don't even know you, nor do I have any pull with my boss. I screwed up, remember?"

"I remember, but still, there are plenty of other agents in the FBI my boss could have chosen."

"Did you screw up?" she asked, taking a sip of her drink.

"What?" He hadn't screwed up. He'd been pursuing his cases in the gung ho way he always did. All except the Ghost's case. That was something he was pursuing under the guise of his FBI job, but was really much more personal to him. His supervisor had never really come out and said he should drop the Ghost's case. It got him to thinking this bodyguard assignment with Rio had come at a crucial point in his investigation. Was he seeing a conspiracy theory where there wasn't one?

"Maybe you treaded on somebody's toes and this is your punishment."

"Rio, I'm on a sun-drenched beach with a beautiful

woman for a two-week walk-in-the-park assignment. Where is the punishment?"

Rio bent over to rummage around in her bag and Max almost swallowed his tongue. The globes of her breasts sidled together to form cleavage he couldn't take his eyes off even if his life depended on it.

"You do have a point there," she said casually as if she wasn't giving him the peep show of his life. "But I'm tired of thinking and worrying about what happened," she continued, shoving and searching through her bag.

Each time she moved, her firm, round breasts danced and bounced. He licked his dry lips. "Can't we just take a break from all this and enjoy some time on the government's dime?" He watched as her silky auburn hair slid along her shoulder and dropped down into that sweet cleft between her breasts. His heart rate accelerated and he started to sweat.

Damn she was sweet, such a visceral addiction, all heat, the taste and feel and scent of her imprinted on every fantasy he'd had, which was driving him insanely crazy.

Today had been such a tease, to be with her and meet the challenge of keeping his desires and his imagination in check. He'd done a pretty poor job of it. Every inch of bare skin had made him want to run his tongue over her to make a connection, to get her wet and mark her as his…the side of her neck, the tender inside of her wrist, the expanse of bare leg in that schoolgirl skirt. He wanted his mouth on her everywhere.

It was a conquest thing, meeting the challenge,

and she was such an exquisite challenge. Yeah, he knew the goal. He understood what was happening between them.

It was like he wanted to meld with her, but he wasn't a guy who "melded." He was a guy who conquered.

Okay, it was a little crazy how much he'd thought about her, how much he wanted her, and there was nothing about the fact that had made him happy. His life was all about control, and wanting something he couldn't have did not fit the paradigm.

But here she was, flashing him, and he'd gotten hard. *Rock-solid hard.*

Finally, she found what she was looking for and straightened. She slipped the sunglasses on her face and looked at him expectantly.

He was supposed to answer, supposed to form words and do what humans had been doing for centuries—communicate.

"Okay," he heard himself say as if the logical, quick-witted part of him had separated from his primal part. One syllable words. This was going downhill fast.

But not all of it was his fault. The water lapped against the beach in an erotic push-pull of waves, the palm trees swayed in the soft, gentle wind. He was standing in a freaking postcard for a sex-filled vacation. He was truly outnumbered and outmanned by an auburn-haired vixen with a glorious body and an intriguing personality.

Right. He was thinking about her personality right now.

He watched as a waiter walked up to her and asked her for her drink order. The waiter's eyes lingered on her breasts and sidled down her torso and her legs. Max wanted to sink his fist into the smiling bastard's face for even looking at her.

Quite the revelation for a man who prided himself on relying on quick thinking and fast reflexes rather than the use of brutality when it came to problem solving in tricky situations.

And he'd been in her presence for less than twenty-four hours.

After she ordered a virgin piña colada, she looked over at him. "Do you want something, Max?"

Did he want something? He wanted everything. He remembered what it had been like to kiss her and he wanted that again.

He remembered what it had been like to touch her, the feel of her hot, wet desire against the sensitive pad of his fingers. How could he forget that?

What he wanted to experience was how she'd feel naked in his arms. Ah, he bet she'd be so freaking soft, and so incredibly hot. The whole short interlude in the plane's lavatory was permanently hardwired into his memory banks—and there she was, not three feet away, smelling like exotic perfume, in a red string bikini, with her hair coming undone.

"Max," she said, pulling down the sunglasses so she would have an unobstructed view of his meltdown.

She was so unexpected. Her eyes were clear and guileless and such a pure jewel-like amber, her skin so satiny, her hair an awesome shade of auburn that caught the sun and burst into flame…everything about her so polished and just so.

"Whiskey, straight. The good stuff," he said, eyeing the waiter.

There wasn't a namby-pamby umbrella drink that would take care of what he needed now.

Rio gave him one last look and pushed her sunglasses back up her nose.

Max squeezed a generous amount of sun lotion in his hand and finished the job of protecting his skin. With a muttered curse he said, "I'm going for a dip."

Unfortunately when he hit the ocean waves, the water was a balmy 81 degrees and didn't cool him off one bit. He should have requested they go to a mountain retreat. No, that wouldn't have been any good, either. Then there would have been a roaring fire, and with the cold there would have been too much of that trying-to-keep-warm business, which would lead to snuggling and other things that generated body heat.

When he got back to where Rio lounged, she was sipping from a tall glass with a little pink umbrella stuck in it. She glanced up at him and smiled. He picked up the whiskey on the side table of the cabana chair, the liquid the same color as her eyes, and downed the whole contents in one burning swallow.

"You okay?"

"Couldn't be better," he said. He walked over, snagged another chair and dragged it to where she was. The beach boy brought him a towel and Max dried off quickly and sank down in the chair. He reached for his discarded shirt, stripped his sunglasses out of the breast pocket and slipped them on.

"You're not really a vacation type of guy, are you?"

"What do you mean?"

"Okay, I'll spell it out. You're a workaholic, right?"

"No. I'm not. I put in my time, but I take time for fun."

She snorted. "Your overtime, you mean."

"I can have fun when it's the right time. I just chafe at being pulled away from open cases."

"You mean your pursuit of the Ghost."

"What do you know about it?"

"I got briefed. I know what happened to your sister. She was quite courageous, I might add."

"Yes, she was amazing and I almost lost her because of the Ghost. You don't remember anything about him that could be helpful?"

"No, I'm sorry. I wish I could remember."

"How about giving me some details on how your mission went wrong?" When he saw her stiffen, he held up his hands. "I'm not asking for any mission specifics, Rio, just what happened to you and how it came about you saw the Ghost."

She was debating. He could see that by the way she worked at her bottom lip with her teeth. He also knew when she made a decision because she took off her sunglasses and looked at him.

"All right, but please don't ask me any mission particulars. I can't…"

"Divulge. I understand."

"I found Eduardo Fuentes's compound late at night. I didn't know it was his at first until I got closer. I figured it would be a good idea to scout the area before I continued on my way."

"Reconnaissance can save your life," Max said.

"Yes, I can vouch for that. Anyway, I was tired. I had been up for twenty-four hours, most of that moving over tough terrain. I found what I thought was a good place to lie low until the sun came up and I could make my way around the compound and get to my destination."

"I wouldn't second-guess that call, Rio."

"What makes you think I'm second-guessing it?"

"Just a hunch," Max said.

"Okay, so I am. I'm thinking I should have just continued on my way. Working around the perimeter in the dark surely wasn't optimal, but I could have done it."

"Sure, and you could have walked into a booby trap or encountered a guard. It was a good call."

"Are you always so sure of yourself?" Rio asked.

"Yes."

She laughed as he'd meant her to because he knew how dangerous field work could be.

"How do you know so much about moving through a jungle in the dead of night?"

"I was a marine. I've been in more deserts than jungles, though."

"Mmm, a few good men. Are you good?"

"I am."

She gave him a soft smile. "Anyway, I found a suitable place and bunked for the rest of the night. When I woke up, it was still very dark. I realized I was on the very edge of the compound, but I'd hidden myself well. Well enough to see one of the balconies overlooking the compound. There were two men standing there talking.

I pulled out my binoculars and when I focused in, I was overjoyed. It was Fuentes. The other man I didn't know, but he…he looked so familiar to me."

"Familiar? How so?"

RIO KNEW SHE HAD to be careful here. She really hadn't seen the man's face enough to identify him for the DEA, but Max didn't know that and he couldn't know that. It was the lie she was telling to keep him occupied and fill out her cover story. She hated the duplicity, but she had no choice. She was here duping Max because her boss had told her that a DEA agent's life hung in the balance.

"He was in shadow and in profile, but something about him made me think I'd seen him before. Unfortunately, I just can't remember anything important about his features."

That seemed to appease Max. The next part of her story was all true and she wished she didn't have to run the events of her capture through her mind ever again.

"Is it possible during one of your past missions, you came into contact with the Ghost and, of course, didn't know it?" Max asked.

She shivered. In all the times she'd relived those events, over and over again, awake and in endless nightmares, she'd never once contemplated that possibility.

"It's possible," she agreed. "I've been on many drug raids and dealt with many shady and dangerous people. It was probably where I'd seen the man Eduardo Fuentes was talking to. Fuentes let it slip that his guest, the shadowy man on the balcony, was in fact the Ghost."

"Fuentes told you the man was the Ghost?"

"He didn't mean to and I'll get to that."

"Please, continue."

She closed her eyes to gather her composure. That was an out-and-out lie she was telling. She couldn't be sure that the man on the balcony was the Ghost. He could have been the Ghost's lackey for all she knew.

They flew open when her waiter placed a platter of fruit on the side table between them. "Would you like anything else? We're closing up for the night."

"No, thank you," Rio said. The waiter nodded and disappeared. In fact the little cove they'd settled in was quite empty. Most of the hotel guests had gone inside for dinner.

"Help yourself," Rio said.

"Not right now. I want to hear the rest, Rio."

She nodded. "This is the part of the story where you have to promise me you won't laugh."

"Laugh? Jeez, Rio. You're in that much danger and you think I'll laugh at you."

"You haven't heard the rest yet, have you?"

"No, but I can't imagine you think I'd be amused at any part of this story," Max said.

"Do you know anything about howler monkeys?"

"What?"

"Just answer the question."

"Not really."

"They're red, of course, and not usually aggressive. They make this roaring noise and live in the canopy. I also need to mention I'm a bit afraid of monkeys. In fact, I am downright terrified of them."

"I don't like where this is going."

"You'll like it even less when you hear. One jumped

on me straight from the tree I was standing next to. It lost its balance after it hit me and made a terrible noise as it went down."

"What did you do?"

"I screamed so loud the angels in heaven probably looked around trying to figure out where that noise came from."

"So if it hit heaven, then I'm sure Fuentes's men heard you," Max said.

"They sure did."

This was where she expected him to laugh, but he didn't. He looked at her for a moment, then rose and crossed to her chair. He sat down next to her and took her hand. "I'm going to be honest with you. I've never encountered a monkey and I have to say I'm not particularly fond of them. But if one jumped on me in a tense situation, I can't say I wouldn't have screamed like a little girl."

"Screamed like a little girl?" she queried, trying to hide her sudden amusement.

He held her gaze, and then said, "With pigtails."

She laughed then, and felt her heart contract and expand. The sensation was delightful and disturbing, as well. With the reality of why she was really here in such an idyllic spot with such a tempting, tantalizing man, she should say something intentionally provocative and flirtatious. She should because the probable outcome of the mission she was on, and the fact only one of them was going to be getting what they wanted, wasn't exactly conducive to forming any kind of ongoing relationship. So to deflect and seduce, enjoy what they could have and be happy with that, would certainly be the wise course of action. It was certainly the course of action she'd always expected herself to take in such a situation.

She'd already suffered enough loss—her parents, Shane. Putting her heart on the line seemed just too dangerous to her, ironic really. So she didn't do serious relationships.

"Why do you think the monkey jumped on you?"

"I don't know. Maybe it thought I was part of the tree. I was dressed in camo. I'll never forget the look on its face. When I screamed and jumped away from it, my feet got tangled in the undergrowth and I fell. If I hadn't been incapacitated, I swear I would have run for the hills."

"Maybe he thought you were another howler monkey with all this red hair."

She laughed again and didn't know how he did it, but she suspected the next time she thought about this incident, she'd do so with more humor and less fear.

"So they caught you."

"Yes. Hit me so hard I blacked out. As I was coming to, that's when I heard Fuentes say they had better not have killed me because he wanted answers as to who I was and why I was there. He said he didn't want the Ghost inconvenienced and was expecting a weapons shipment. That's all I heard before I blacked out again. At least, it's what I thought I heard."

"Come here," he said, reaching over and tugging on her arm.

"What?"

"You're too far away. This can't be easy for you," he said, pulling her across his lap and shifting back until he was the one with his back against the canvas of the cabana chair. He pulled the canopy over them. Her side rested against his bare chest. "Much better." He leaned down and pressed a kiss to her temple. "I know it doesn't count for much, but I don't like dragging you through this, either."

It was all so much—unburdening herself, trying to reconcile having someone else understand what she went through, then this…this overload of sensations with him holding her, caring about her… "I can handle this," she said while not making the least effort to climb out of his lap.

"I know you can. You took on a howler monkey and lived to tell the tale."

She groaned. "I'm never going to live this down, am I?"

"Far be it from me to tease you about the monkey, Rio. I think what you went through and how you're dealing with it is admirable."

She trembled a little, wanted to be strong enough to scoot away, but had the presence of mind to finally admit to herself this felt good. Having someone on her side didn't just have to mean physical support. It meant emotional support, too. And her world wouldn't come to an end if she admitted she needed a little of that right now.

"I'm not used to this, Max," she said. "And I find it's too easy to lean. I'm not the leaning type, but that doesn't mean I don't appreciate the support." She turned so she could look more fully at him. "Now that you know more than the DEA, are you happy?"

"How is that?"

"I didn't tell them about the monkey. I couldn't. I just told them a guard saw the gleam off my binoculars and caught me. So now you know one of my most humiliating stories."

"I'll go to the grave with it," he said.

"You will? My hero."

With that, he leaned closer and captured her mouth. And that felt pretty damn good, too. How he had gone from complete stranger to this in such a short time, she had no idea. But he was here. And, for now, she liked it that way. Enough to kiss him back.

And despite the fatigue, the stress, the pain—or maybe because of it—their passion quickly got out of hand. And she did absolutely nothing to stop it. There was so much left to be said, so much more to go through, and this felt so very, very good. There wasn't enough of this in her world, and she, quite greedily, decided to take it now that it was here.

They broke apart and, spying the fruit on the table, Rio reached for a strawberry. She was suddenly and inexplicably hungry. She bit into the fruit and juice escaped her mouth and dribbled down her chin. But the flesh of the fruit didn't do anything to slake her hunger. The flesh she craved to touch and explore was so close and so warm all she had to do was reach out and take it.

He picked up a slice of pineapple and bit into the sweet, firm fruit.

"This is good," he said. "You should try it." He

offered her the fruit but Rio fused her mouth to his and stole the piece inside. He groaned deep in his throat.

"Mmm," she hummed, licking her lips with the tip of her pink tongue.

Something inside Max gave way. The red-tinged sky made her look rosy, turning her bikini a deeper shade. "Rio," he said softly.

Her lids seemed heavy as she opened her eyes, glittering in the fading light like fireflies.

She moved from sitting astride his lap to straddling him, and his hands moved to her back, to those tantalizing strings. Two quick pulls and the top simply wasn't there anymore. In the position he was in, it was easy for him to help himself to the very tight tips of her nipples.

He took his sweet time paying almost reverent attention to first one, then the other, turgid tip. She wriggled her hips and gasped as his mouth moved over each nipple.

Using his tongue, he licked at her, the pineapple still in his hand. He rubbed it over the hard points until Rio cried out, panting softly in the night air.

He latched onto her again, biting and licking the juice from her nipples. The taste was tart and sweet on his tongue.

Her soft moans, and the gasps every time he so much as breathed, told him she was in as heightened a state of awareness as he was. It was exactly want he wanted.

He wanted her to respond to him on the most basic level, trying to trick himself into thinking everything with this woman was just sexual.

He'd imagined it wild and tender, carnal and sweet, a

roller coaster of sensation, emotion and primal responses, where barriers of any kind could no longer exist.

"This isn't going to be simple," he murmured.

"That's the problem. You'll have expectations. I don't know that I can fulfill any of them. I don't know what you want beyond this moment and I can't make you any promises."

"I don't recall asking for any. One step at a time, okay? Not everything has to be planned out."

"I just—" She stopped. "Okay." She smiled sweetly.

He tugged her close, bumped hips with her, making her eyes widen a little. "You can tell I don't mind in the least." He slid a hand beneath the heavy hair at her nape and brought her head down. "Maybe tonight you'll have sweet dreams. If I can do that, it's enough." He kissed her then, and put all the promise he felt behind it— things he couldn't yet put words to. And when she kissed him back, so easily, so honestly, his own barriers began to crumble, ones he hadn't even been aware were there. By the time he'd broken the kiss, he felt compelled to say, "Okay, so I wasn't entirely truthful."

She frowned. "In what way?"

"I don't think it'll be enough. I want to know all there is to know about you. Your favorite food, what position you like best in bed, what you're still not telling me about Fuentes."

"Max—"

"I can try to promise to be patient, but I'm afraid that'll end up being something I won't be able to pull off, either. But I'll sure give it a try." He kissed her again, until she was making those soft moans that made him crazy. Then he slid his hands down over her hips, thrusting upward to make contact with his rock-hard length.

She was kissing him back, greedily, squeezing her knees, pulling him toward her.

"Hold on," he told her, wrapping one arm around her back, the other closing around her nape, keeping her mouth fused to his as he rose. "Ever done it in the surf?"

4

As dusk deepened into night, voices had them both on the alert. Company was the last thing Rio wanted. When she met Max's eyes, she could see it was also something he was very much against.

He moved them around to the end of the cove in a secluded place where water collided with smooth black rock.

He let her legs slip free as sun-warmed water lapped around their ankles, slapped against their calves, thighs and torsos.

Before she could even register the warm rock against her back, her thoughts scattered instantly as his lips closed around one aching tip.

She gasped and arched into him, the exquisite sensations spearing through her, rendering her speechless as well as mindless.

"You taste pretty damn good."

She was focusing on trying to keep herself from sliding down the rock wall into a puddle at his feet. Pleasure shot through her, from the tips of her breasts, like an arrow straight down between her thighs.

He hooked his fingers around the string of her

bikini bottoms and tugged. Slowly. Excruciatingly slowly.

She wanted to tip her head back and close her eyes, and just focus on feeling every sensation. But she couldn't take her eyes off him. She tried not to tremble so hard, but she couldn't seem to stop. The warm water sheeted across her naked torso, tapping her aching nipples, sliding across her skin, drenching his hair, dripping off his jaw, as he continued baring her skin to his intently focused gaze.

Her thighs quivered in anticipation of his touch. Even with the water spraying and splashing, she could feel his warm breath brush against her oh-so-sensitive skin. She wanted to sink her fingers into his hair, urge him closer, urge him to please put an end to the torturous wait. But he continued pushing her bikini bottoms down her thighs, over her calves, slipping his palms up one leg to help dislodge first one foot, then the other.

And now she was naked to him. He slid his hands slowly along the front of her shins, then around the backs of her knees and slowly up her thighs, nudging them apart, just slightly.

She sighed as, once again, his breath fanned across her inner thighs. She thought she'd scream if he didn't stop there, and finally he slowly drew his tongue along her most sensitive flesh. Part whimper, part moan slipped from her mouth.

He grabbed her hands when she tried to urge him on and settled her tighter against the gently sloping rock that made a perfect, firm surface to the hard planes of his body. He drew her hands over her head and went back to his ministrations.

But she was much too restless to leave her hands crossed above her head.

"Be good," he whispered in her ear as his hard chest pressed thick and strong against her aching breasts. He moved down her body, sucking on her nipple as he eased from the aching tip to her quivering abdomen and finally to her groin. With his big palms, he pressed her legs open, his head dipping down, down until…contact with her aching flesh.

She placed her palms flat against the rock to brace herself against the roiling surf and Max's clever and delicious tongue.

She arched her back when he found her pulsing clit and circled it with his tongue, burning her with wet flicks and slow, soft swirls.

His groan was audible above the sound of the surf as he leaned in closer, his unshaven cheek scraped her thigh and his breath burst over her sex.

Stab after stab of pleasure trembled through her, building with each movement of his tongue over her sensitive, burning clit.

"Max," she gasped as water cascaded over them. His tongue never stopped its delicious assault as moans poured out of her in uncontrollable succession. One last splash of water against her aching nipples and the hard, sucking movement of Max's mouth sent Rio over the edge to a white-hot burst of passion that made her hips buck and her back arch away from the smooth rock.

He slid up her body, bracing her between himself and the rock as he trailed his lips over her torso, pushing her hands up again and linking his fingers through hers as he pressed them on either side of her head.

Water plumed up and over them in a gentle fall of droplets that helped to cool her exposed skin, but where Max pressed burned as hot as the once-active volcano that had formed this island.

"Man, Max, you…" She couldn't seem to form coherent words, her thoughts scattered like the spray that sheeted over them in rhythm with the ebb and flow of the surf.

"Shh," he told her, then pulled her arms down around his neck, tipped her chin up and kissed her.

It was confident, certain and seductive. He didn't just kiss her lips, he feasted on them, and every touch and taste was an invitation for her to do the same. That was something she was starting to get used to about him. It was clear he wanted a partner in pleasure and that relieved some of her tension. Sex she could do. That was all she could do. She was a strong, confident woman, both in and out of bed. She could quench Max's desire with her body, but if he ever wanted more… Well, she was done with that.

She'd been through too much, lost too much to ever go down that road again.

His gentle mouth turned urgent, making her feel both needed and wanted at the same time. He tucked his hips against hers, still kissing her deeply, twining his tongue along hers as he pulled her thighs up over his hips, pinning her to the rock. "Rio…" he murmured against her lips. "I don't want to stop, but—"

"Then don't." She buried her fingers in his wet curls and tugged his mouth back to hers. She should use this opportunity to move away, to set boundaries, but she wanted him.

"Protection," he said, his body tensing as she hooked her heels behind his thighs.

"I'm safe," she said. "It's okay."

He lifted his head, looked her in the eyes. "Are you sure?"

"Very."

His eyes were so dark, so intense. And it was all in want of her. A heady rush raced through her all over again.

"Rio—"

"I'm protected. And I'm safe. And I want you…deep inside me. Right now." She was aroused, sexually needy. That was all, she told herself. It didn't have anything to do with *this* particular man.

She pushed away the promise she made never to lie to herself.

That feeling, that need, was as thrilling as it was intimidating. But now she wasn't going to worry about it. Right now, all she wanted to feel was him taking her. He needed no more coaxing as he slid slowly, fully and completely inside her.

"Hold on tight," he commanded, the words more growl than anything.

She didn't hesitate to comply with his demand. She dug her fingers into his shoulders and locked her ankles more tightly behind him as he eased her higher on the rock so she could angle her hips upward…and thrust. His broad palms covered her hips, guiding her down onto him. She arched and moaned when he began to move faster.

She clung to him, both of them grunting as his thrusts grew deeper, faster. She wanted to take things more slowly and hang on to the moment as long as she could, but he was thrusting into her and she could only give herself over to it, to the powerful emotions rushing through her.

This is just sex, she tried telling herself firmly. Against her will she felt a bond forming, but she pushed it out of her mind.

And then whatever thoughts she had scattered completely as he slowed, and she could feel his body coil, tense, pull back, all in preparation for what she knew was coming. It was enough to send her over, water pounding against her sweat-slicked torso, as she gasped for air and gave back equally with every thrust he made.

He cried out when he came, his fingers digging into her hips in a way she knew would leave marks…marks so much different than the ones on her ribs. She gave herself over to him, reveled in his shuddering release, tightening around him to give him every last drop of pleasure.

He was shaking as he slid from her body and let her legs drop from around his waist. He held her tightly against him as they both fought for breath.

It was several minutes before she came back to herself. Max made no move to leave, or to let her go. And she made no move, either. Their heartbeats eased to a somewhat steadier rhythm. It was the only thing steady about her just then.

It felt better than she could have imagined in his arms. Held so tightly, both cuddled and coddled. It wasn't like her to accept this level of closeness from anyone, most especially in an instance like this when she was here in his arms under false pretenses. She fought so long and hard for her independence, it had carried over to all aspects of her personal and professional life, including intimacy. So why she so willingly accepted his protection, his surprising gentleness, she had no idea. She chalked it up to the moment…and to her painful past.

It was a whirlwind of activity to get from the secluded cove back to their cabana chair and belongings, and then through the hotel to their room.

After they had showered together, with more touching and exploration than she'd ever experienced with a man before, it was time to dry off.

"That was…" He let the words trail off, but held her gaze, his own intensifying in ways that had her heart rate kicking up again.

"Yeah," she said softly. "It was."

He gathered her closer, settling her between his legs, so she was pressed against the full length of him, chest to chest, hip to hip. The soft places of her meeting all the hard planes of him. It felt remarkably fantastic…and far too perfect. She never wanted to leave…but she knew it was inevitable. Two weeks was only two weeks and Fuentes was still out there, still the man who had murdered her stepbrother, Shane. She intended to bring him in dead or alive.

Max rested his chin on her head, and she took the easy way out, nuzzling his chest, keeping their gazes disconnected a little while longer. She didn't want to risk him seeing anything in her eyes, especially when she hadn't sorted it herself just yet.

"How about some dinner?"

Thankful for the casual question, she nudged him in his ribs. "Men. It's either food or sex."

"Throw in some sports and you've got us pegged."

"I think what we did on those rocks constitutes a sport, my friend. I think that I'm going to feel like I've been in a football game and I was the ball." She shifted in his arms, felt the soreness all over her body and laughed lightly. "Or maybe now."

"I'll make you a deal," he said, pulling back the curtain and snagging towels.

He dangled one in front of her with a smile and she grabbed at it, stepping onto the bath mat. Max slipped a towel around his waist and secured the end. "What would that be?" She reached for a smaller towel and began squeezing the water out of her hair. She felt satisfied, drowsy and contented, and hoped that the mood between them would stay that way. She'd like this fantasy she was experiencing to go on just a little bit longer.

He whipped the towel out of her hands and nudged her around so her back was to him. He rubbed at her hair to get out the excess water.

She felt too comfortable in this intimate role. To alleviate the tension she suddenly felt building in her stomach, she pulled the towel out of his hands and wrapped it around her head.

Max was just too easy to be with. He bent down and kissed the curve of her neck.

Dangerous thinking, but that's what Max Carpenter did to her.

She sighed and leaned back into him, knowing she could so easily trust this man. She shored up her defenses.

"How about room service?" Max said, lifting her hair and kissing her nape, sending a delicious tingling sensation skittering over her skin. "And I'll see what I can do to relax those mystery muscles later."

If only it were that simple: playing house in the vacation capital of the South Pacific.

A cozy, intimate dinner in their room? Not something Rio could handle right now, especially given how vulnerable he was making her feel. Dammit, he wasn't going to do this to her. She would stay in control. She would complete her mission to keep him occupied. She had a job to do and she would start thinking about that.

"I'd rather dine in the dining room."

"I don't know, Rio. The fact that you think you saw someone you recognized has stayed in the back of my mind. It might be safer here in the room. After all, I'm here to keep you safe."

They had only been in Maui for about five hours and staying here and losing more of the battle with herself wasn't a smart move. But his words brought back the memory of being in the lobby when she thought she'd recognized the man going into the elevator. A flash of a cheekbone, large fists slamming into her sides, bones cracking and she pulled in on herself. Suddenly, she wondered about her competency. Had that man been one of the goons who had pummeled her and kept her captive?

"What is it you're not telling me?" he asked.

Her heart skipped a beat. She couldn't admit to herself she wasn't competent to make a call about the man she thought she'd seen. The DEA and making Fuentes pay were all she had. He'd taken Shane.

Then Max slipped his finger beneath her chin and turned her gaze to his when she looked away in a vain effort to regroup. "Is something wrong?" he asked, never more sincere, real concern outlined in every inch of his handsome face. "Tell me and we can deal with it together."

For a split second she wanted to unburden herself and tell him everything, lean on him and trust him. But after everything she'd lost, she couldn't take that chance with Max. She didn't do together anymore. Believing in other people was for suckers. She was strictly a solo act now. "No," she said flatly and pointedly extricated herself from the tight space he'd cornered her into. "I'm more than capable of taking care of myself, but thank you ever so kindly for your concerns. In fact I want to go to dinner and I want to wear the cute white sundress the DEA so generously provided. I'm not helpless or one of your normal assignments, Max. So let's go."

She didn't wait for him, but stepped out of his arms and through the bathroom door with a deliberate calm that cost her more than he'd ever realize.

Less than two weeks with him and it was going to be an internal battle for her all the way.

MAX STOOD IN THE now-empty, steamy bathroom, wondering what in the hell had just happened, once again.

One second her barriers had fallen, revealing something quite surprisingly vulnerable beneath that confident surface. The next moment, not only were the barriers wholly back in place, but they'd also been reinforced with a fair amount of anger. But he had no idea what he'd said to provoke it.

He knew she had a lot of pride in her abilities, which had been well earned, he was sure. He hadn't thought she'd bristle quite so ardently at the mere suggestion that they eat in the room where it was safer. And he started to wonder if he hadn't been right on target from the beginning about this babysitting assignment.

He'd had a sense there was a lot more to it than a protection detail and he couldn't shake the thought she might have an alternative agenda, either DEA-sanctioned or not. He didn't enjoy that feeling, especially when he particularly liked the woman, but he played back over the time just after his offer. He might not understand the rest, but he needed no additional clarification for that particular moment. There had been something quite…exposed in the expression that had crossed her face. He had absolutely no doubt he'd hit on something there. The question was, what was it?

What he did know was there was more going on here for her than her hiding from the Ghost.

The image of her face, her eyes, the way her lips had instinctively parted when he'd asked her what she'd left unsaid, played through his mind again. And again. There had been both fear and yearning in her eyes. Whatever it was, for a second there, or two, she'd wanted to tell him.

So he dressed in one of his loud shirts and a pair of jeans and took her down to the restaurant.

He walked with her to a table and tried to seat her, but she pulled out her own chair with a defiant look at him and sat down, daring him to comment.

He wasn't giving up, not even close, but she was clearly in retreat and regroup mode. Pushing someone when they're scrambling often worked to break down that resistance, at least enough to get them to the point where they'd ask for help. He knew with someone like Rio, it would only make her rebuild those defenses twice as fast, and make them twice as sturdy. Now was the time to back off and do a little regrouping of his own.

He pulled a roll from a basket that was set on the table and once she gave her drink order, he gave the waiter his.

"I saw in the brochure there's quite a lot to see along the Hana Road. Want to rent a car tomorrow and drive it?"

Rio shrugged. "That sounds like a good idea. I've felt confined too long."

"Makes me antsy, too. I'm not one for inaction."

"You're pretty good on the action stuff, Carpenter," she said, leaning forward.

Max settled back in his seat, only partly relieved to be on solid footing again. The rest of him was still stuck in the steamy bathroom and their disturbing conversation.

He held her gaze. "The best."

The waiter brought her a glass of wine and him more bourbon. Maybe he'd taken everything his boss had told him too much on its merits and ignored his instincts too long. He was tempted to contact Drew Miller or Callie to dig a little deeper on Rio Marshall. He decided against it. He didn't want anyone or anything intruding on this time, at least until he got a better personal handle on it.

The waiter delivered their dinners—succulent seafood platters, filled with lobster and scallops.

"Don't worry, Max. I'm not going to skip out on you. I know I can take care of myself, but the DEA put me here and I'm not going to jeopardize my job by being stubborn."

"I'd find you, Rio. Wherever you went. That's a promise. I, too, take my job seriously."

Rio mulled that over as she chewed a chunk of lobster, then sipped her wine. "Noted. But you really don't have to worry."

Max was distracted by her lips, but diverted his attention back to the discussion as soon as he realized what he was doing. "What I worry about when I'm on an assignment is lack of information. Not getting the full story can compromise your mission or, worse, get you killed."

She took another bite, sucking on the buttered lobster chunk she'd put in her mouth, and Max watched her face for any telltale sign, but she'd obviously regrouped as her expression didn't give him any clues.

It was damn frustrating to watch her eat as he tried to keep his mind on what they were talking about, all the while gazing at her mouth doing something as innocent as sucking on buttered seafood. He'd never wanted so badly to be a lump of lobster.

Concentrate.

"I don't intend to cause anyone's death, unless, of course, I have to defend myself. Satisfied?"

She licked her slick lips and Max had to wonder if she was being intentionally provocative. Or was it the fact anything this woman did turned him on?

"No, not yet, but I'm trying not to remember that you're a bit sore."

She glanced at him then, only there was no amusement to be found in her stare. For some perverse reason, that made him smile anyway. He wondered what she'd say if he told her she was quite cute when she was irritated, but figured that would only get him the silent treatment. Or possibly shot.

"There's way too much of an audience for me," she said archly.

Before he could answer, her eyes went steely and she pushed back from the table. "We've got to go."

"Why?"

"He's found me."

She pulled Max out of the restaurant and took the elevator at a run. Once inside, she punched the number to their floor.

"What's going on?

"It was the Ghost's man I saw. He's here and that can only mean one thing."

"What?"

"One of our agencies does have a mole and that traitor pointed the Ghost in our direction. How else could he know where I was going to be?"

Max pulled out his cell. "Let me call the FBI."

"No, Max," Rio said, grabbing his arm. "Don't you understand? We can't trust either agency. If it gets back to the mole, they'll know where we've gone. No. We have to do this on our own."

"Why are we going up?"

"I've got to get my flee bag. We need it, and then we can go. It'll only take a minute."

They were out of the elevator in a flash. Rushing

down the hall, Rio swiped her card to enter the room. The second the door opened, a meaty fist sank into her hair and dragged her forward.

Max barreled in to find Rio struggling with a man who pointed a gun at him. Caught flat-footed, Max froze. Rio brought up her knee into the man's crotch, but he dodged, so she grabbed on to his balls and jerked. He yowled in pain. Preoccupied with Rio's viselike grip on his jewels, he dropped the gun and grabbed for her hand, allowing Max to surge forward and plant his fist into the man's face.

As soon as he was down, Rio didn't hesitate for an instant. She grabbed her backpack and then Max's hand. Racing from the hotel room, they ran down the hall toward the elevator, but saw it light up and ding. Changing direction, she hit the door to the stairs and they raced down them at a breakneck speed.

Max heard shouting and soon bullets followed, causing mortar to fly as they ducked and continued to run.

Exploding out of the doors, they ran for the dock. Quickly, they jumped aboard a boat and Rio made quick work of getting it started. They were off, moving so fast water sprayed up over the hull.

Max thought they had gotten away until he heard gunshots and realized the thugs had a boat waiting. No, make that two.

"Hurry, Rio. We've got company."

"It's at full throttle."

Max hesitated, thinking they would outrun them, but then he saw the missile launcher and his mouth went dry.

The sound of the small missile leaving the tube whistled through the night. Max leaped for Rio and their world exploded.

5

THE SOLID WEIGHT of Max propelled her over the side of the boat into the water. Because they'd been traveling at top speed, the impact jarred her, twisting them around in the wake left by the rushing speedboat. Disoriented in the black water, Rio tried to get her bearings as her body finally settled, allowing her to kick for the surface.

Her battered body ached in new places, her bruised ribs throbbing in time to her heartbeat. Coming up for air, Rio ignored the pain and looked frantically around. When she saw Max's body floating on top of the water, her heart stopped. She swam to him and flipped him over. He was breathing, but he had a cut on his head that told her he took the brunt of the explosion.

Grabbing Max in a swimmer's hold, she turned to make her way back to Maui. Two boats circled the burning speedboat, but Rio moved quickly when the light flashed their way. With any luck, they'd think she and Max were dead and move on.

"What the hell happened?" Max asked when he came to.

"Your quick thinking got us away from those thugs. They're still searching for us."

Max studied the scene, the fire on the speed boat still sending up flames and oily smoke. The smell of gas was heavy on the water.

"Are you okay to swim?" Rio asked.

"Yes. My head hurts, but it's not bad enough to keep me from dry land."

Rio nodded and followed Max as he headed toward the beach. She was convinced those were Eduardo Fuentes's men. What chilled her was they wanted her alive. They could have killed her easily, either in the hotel room or by aiming directly at their boat. Instead, they had targeted the engine.

What could he possibly want with her?

Guilt washed over Rio. She should tell Max the truth about why he was "babysitting" her, but she was under strict orders to not compromise the undercover DEA's mission.

She didn't like lying to Max, but that's the way it would have to be.

When she hit the beach only moments after Max, her legs felt like rubber. Her pretty white dress with the colorful fish was ruined and she was soaked to the bone. But she'd managed to snag her backpack, and that meant everything she'd stashed in the waterproof liners survived.

She didn't have a moment to catch her breath. Bullets chipped at the sand, sending little puffs up, the sound like a sizzling zing in her ears.

Rio burst into motion. Grabbing on to Max's hand, she propelled them forward. They pelted up a black sand hillock, through lush undergrowth, until they crouched in a copse of trees.

"The other boat has hit the sand. We're in for a fight unless we get the heck out of here."

"Agreed." Rio looked around and saw nothing but wilderness. No lights, no illumination, nothing but darkness.

"I want you to wait here. I'll lead them off. Don't move from this position or I'll never find you in the dark."

She gave him a quick nod. Fear for his safety caused a tight knot to form in her stomach. She grabbed his wrist before he took off. "Be careful, Max."

At the doubt in her voice, his brows thickened with a frown. "Military guy, remember? Now, let me see your mean face."

She chuckled even with the threat all around them. She searched his face, liking the man beneath the tough-as-nails exterior. He trusted her. Right now he was laying his life on the line for her and guilt was a bad taste in her mouth. "Kick ass, Max, and don't worry about taking names."

His features smoothed, and there was tenderness in his voice. "That's better. I will. Remember. Don't move, Rio." He pulled a gun from the waistband of his jeans. "I don't even know if this will work."

"Club them with it, then."

He laughed.

"And if I don't come back…do the best you can."

Max was still standing there. "Go—go, then." She shooed him. "I'll be fine."

He smiled, took a step, then cradled the back of her head and kissed her, hard and fast.

"Whoa. Screw these guys. Let's find a room," Rio said.

He chuckled as he disappeared through the trees. She breathed deep, checked the time and started to dig in her bag for the weapons she'd stored there.

Before she could get to them, out of her peripheral vision she saw a shadow move. Even at this distance, she knew it wasn't Max.

She was trapped with an open area behind her and nothing for cover. She felt the presence seconds before a gun poked her in the ribs.

"Hands up," he said. With the gun, a man motioned her toward the beach.

Rio moved slowly, staying out of arm's reach. "What do you want with me?"

He shrugged indifferently. "That's for Fuentes to decide, *puta*. I just bag 'em." He kept his aim tight on her, circling and forcing her where he wanted her to go. "Where is your bodyguard, *chica?*"

"Bringing up the rear," Max said.

The man spun and Max punched hard. The would-be kidnapper hit the ground like a stone and didn't move.

"That was amazing. Excellent KO," she said, bending to snatch up the downed man's weapon.

Max reached for her, and she fell against him. He squeezed her hard. "Are you okay?" She nodded. "Time to go."

An explosion roared across the small spit of land, shaking the ground and disrupting the birds in the trees. She felt the burst of hot air on the back of her head, smiled and turned to look. Orange fire blazed into the night sky, white smoke turning black and sooty before another explosion ripped the air.

"It's amazing what you can do with the enemy's weapons." Max chuckled. "That will slow them down a bit."

"Let's get out of here," Rio said just as gunfire erupted around them. They turned and ran, and soon they hit a dirt road. Not slowing their momentum at all, Rio headed for the wall of dark green dead ahead.

While East Maui was densely populated, West Maui was not. Being the windward side of the island, it was much too breezy and too rocky to entice large resorts or settlements. According to the map they had checked today, most of this area made up the Ko'olau Nature Preserve. They might as well be in the middle of nowhere.

"Let's keep moving." Her ribs protesting with each step, Rio plunged into the quiet, cool darkness, with Max behind her. She fought her way through the underbrush, adding many more cuts and scratches to her skin. They ran in silence for quite some time, tripping through vines and bushes as creepers clutched at their ankles, her breathing in time with Max's as he stuck to her tail. Sweat beaded on their skin, aggravating the fresh, stinging cuts.

Taking a different direction would give them a fighting chance. She could only hear the sound of rushing water and her own heartbeat in her ears. She froze when she heard gunfire sweep back and forth a ways behind them, then suddenly cease.

She stopped, cautious about falling down a ravine or into a pool of water. It was so dark she could barely see Max. "We need to move slowly. I hear water."

"It could be a waterfall. There are quite a few around here according to the brochure," he said.

Trying to see through the darkness, she took cautious steps. She had flashlights in her pack, but she didn't want to chance using the light this close to their assailants.

"Let's go slow, then. I don't want to take a header off a ravine."

"I don't want to fall, period."

Rio put her hand on his arm to gauge his distance and reassure herself he was as solid as she remembered. "I don't think they're going to chase us while it's dark. It's too dangerous. They'll probably regroup and then come after us when it's full light."

"Sounds reasonable."

"Let's get to the waterfall, and then decide what we're going to do from there."

"You take the lead," Max said, finding and squeezing her arm.

"You know…it's a rare man that gives over the lead to a woman," she said. "Especially in a situation like this."

He smiled, his teeth flashing in the dark. "You've recently been in a jungle. Your skills are more honed. I'll watch your back. It's a great view."

"Me Tarzan, you Jane?"

He chuckled as she started down a steep incline, cautiously placing her sandaled feet. All she needed right now was to twist her ankle. They would surely catch them then.

Rio had climbed a lot of rocks and mountains with nothing but a resin bag and some water. She'd negotiated some of the most dangerous jungles in the Southern Hemisphere, so this trek felt familiar to her.

The trouble was she had to worry about Max. In the past, she'd often worked alone. She slowly and methodically moved down to the base of the incline and encountered a stream. Part of the water sound she'd heard. She waded across the stream to get to the water-fall.

She stepped in the muck in the bottom. It oozed up over the tops of her sandals and lodged between her toes, yet the water felt refreshing on her overheated body. When she hit the other side of the stream, Rio continued along, picking her way until they reached a trail of hard-packed dirt. She followed it toward the rushing water and descended down to the base of the falls.

Rio looked around, a shiver working along her spine. They would be hunted by Fuentes's men without impunity. No law enforcement to help them out.

Max tripped on a root half-buried in the ground and Rio's hand shot out to steady him. Something inside her clenched and released at the feel of his warm skin beneath her palm. Damn, she had wanted to avoid this…this feeling of caring deeply for another person. And now that she cared what happened to Max, she cared how he would feel if he found out she'd been lying to him. He would feel totally betrayed now because they had gotten close, at least physically. But her heart twisted inside her thinking that he would look at her differently. She shifted at the uncomfortable feeling, dreading the look that would come into his eyes. She shook off the feelings, thinking she was going soft. Soon she'd be back on the job fighting bad guys and she was glad of it. At least that endeavor was black and white.

When he stepped into the moonlight, Rio saw the gash on his temple better and her heart tumbled over in her chest. "You're bleeding," she said, her voice husky.

He looked down at her as she pushed wet hair off his forehead to better see the cut, his bright blue eyes penetrating her soul and making her hurt.

He reached up but she nudged his hand away. "I have a first-aid kit in my backpack. Don't touch it."

"Yes, ma'am," he said, giving her a sideways, amused look.

Rio ignored it. She worked at getting herself and her emotions under control. This was a temporary assignment that had clearly turned into something else—both with Max and Fuentes. She didn't know what Eduardo Fuentes wanted with her, but she wasn't going to be bound and gagged and deal with him on his terms. The next time time they met face-to-face, it would be on her terms. That was nonnegotiable.

She unzipped the backpack and pulled out the first-aid kit. She moved back to him with the kit and opened it.

"We're in deep shit here," he said quietly.

"I know," Rio replied, taking a gauze square and soaking it with antiseptic. "I can't trust anyone, not even local law enforcement. I'm truly on my own."

He hissed when she pressed the wet pad to his gash. "Damn, that hurts."

Rio bent forward and blew on it to minimize the sting.

"You're not alone in this, Rio. I'm here and I'm not going to let anything happen to you."

She went still on the outside, but inside things were

happening. Like her heart hitting her rib cage and her stomach fluttering and her blood taking off in a wild race through her system.

"Max, you should really make your way to the hotel and then get back to L.A. The men after me consider you expendable. I won't have you dead because of me." She went to unwrap the butterfly Band-Aid, her hands shaking.

He reached out to grasp her hands, but she stepped back. He took a step closer and she tensed. She tried not to show it, but even that much was really beyond her at this point. The world she lived in made it imperative she make no friends, keep people at a distance. It hurt so much less when they were gone.

"Rio, I know something's not right." He spoke softly, but somehow the tone wasn't the least bit comforting. In fact, it only served to unnerve her further. He saw far too much, far too easily.

"Whether or not that's the case, I'd prefer to handle my own affairs my own way." She put a hand out when he took another step. "Just because we were physical a couple of times doesn't mean I need or want your interference. It's nothing personal. I've been taking care of myself for a long time, and I like it that way."

"So I've gathered." He stopped, but didn't give her an inch.

"I'm not going to change my mind."

He stood his ground and kept his gaze steady on hers. "Just because you don't usually need help doesn't mean you shouldn't consider accepting some when it's offered. I'm guessing that doesn't happen too often."

"Do you do that?" Her hands settled on her hips. "Accept help?"

His gaze shuttered a bit and she realized she'd said exactly the right thing if she wanted him to ease off. "That's what I thought. Please, let's not argue. You should head for the hotel. I'll lie low and work something out. When you get back to L.A.—"

"I'm not leaving you," he growled. He took both of her arms then and pulled her closer. His eyes went hard and flinty, and she had to resist the urge to shiver. "The mole hung us out to dry. *Us,* Rio. They already know who I am." Gone were those smooth-as-velvet pleasant tones. In their place was a flat, steely voice that brooked no argument. "Maybe it's not about what you want but about what you need. You need my help."

"Maybe I don't want to be taken care of."

"So you've said." He gentled his hold, tugging her another step closer. "I know it's hard to accept help from anyone, especially someone you don't know well. I wouldn't have thought I'd get caught up in you. Trust me, I know. I never get involved with anyone, on any side, of anything I view as work-related. You took me by surprise."

"So did you," she replied, without meaning to, which only caused his gaze to intensify, something she hadn't thought possible.

"This innate strength you have, your confidence, your ease with yourself and with everyone else. You command attention without demanding it. You command attention just by being you. You certainly have mine."

She didn't know what to say to that. As a means of getting her to lower her defenses, she had to admit, it was pretty damned effective. Standing this close, looking into his eyes, she saw no sign of deception, no wavering. He was either very, very good at his job, or he was telling her the absolute truth. She wished the stakes on knowing which it was weren't so high.

"I'm dead serious about this, Rio. When I take a job, I follow through on it no matter what. The FBI isn't some alphabet-soup agency to me. I'm loyal and trustworthy to those who earn it."

"So, this is about the job?"

"It was at first, Rio, but now… No. Not now. You have to admit the strength of the attraction between us isn't something to be dismissed. I'm certain the way you responded to me isn't normal for you."

"No…no, that many orgasms aren't normal for me."

The corners of his mouth curved. "Your ability to find even a shred of humor at a time when I know you're not feeling remotely jovial is another draw."

And he drew her. It was what she'd been trying to put into place since he'd walked into the conference room that day. She'd tried to pass it off as a physical thing, a chemistry thing…but it was much more than that. Or she'd have never let him put his hands on her.

"I think nothing gets by you, not even me. Especially not me. You pull no punches, and take no bullshit," he said.

She fought the urge to smile then. How did he do that? Her carefully constructed life was literally falling to pieces…and he was making her smile. Like she had nothing better to do than stand here and flirt. Only this wasn't about flirting. This was about survival.

"How have I earned either of those things from you? You know nothing of what might be going on with me."

"Call it gut instinct." He reached up and tucked a loose strand of hair behind her ear, then very lightly ran his fingertip along her cheekbone and down along her chin.

The brief contact made her so aware of him. He talked about commanding attention. He had no idea.

"You and me are in this together, and together we're going to get out of it. Now let's find some cover," Max said.

"Let me put this on your gash first."

His skin felt warm when she applied the bandage and guilt hit her with the force of a kick to the solar plexus. She still hadn't told him the truth about the men who were after her. For now, their escape would have to take precedence. She'd worry about what to tell Max when they were safe.

Rio started forward and she and Max moved into the thick undergrowth. She breathed a sigh of relief once they got into the dark interior.

"So, we're in the Ko'olau Forest Preserve," Rio said, looking around at the lush surroundings.

"I think so. Farther in it's closed to the public, so it's pretty much deserted. Even if we made it back to Hana, there's not much there except a small town, and a hotel. We're not going to get anywhere near that tiny airport, even if we could get a flight off Maui."

"They're coming after us. I guarantee it. And they're going to be watching all the airports, too."

"And we can't call the FBI or the DEA for fear the mole will be listening in. We're really on our own."

She tugged at her wet dress. "I need to change."

"You have dry clothes in that bag?" Max asked hopefully.

"Yes, I do for both of us. I don't leave anything to chance. And I don't intend to go traipsing through the jungle in a delicate dress and sandals."

"I think I'm going to start calling you Mary Poppins."

"Hey, no joking about my flee bag. Besides, Mary would be good in a fight. She had that umbrella and that spit spot take-no-prisoners attitude."

"Do you have weapons in that bag? I don't mean an umbrella."

"Ha, ye of little faith. Of course I have weapons. Glock—never leave home without it."

"Where exactly are we?"

"Wait, I have a map of Maui."

"Damn, you really are prepared."

"Hey, I've been in tougher jams without all these fun toys and accessories, so when I get a chance to put together some gear, I don't skimp."

She really should make her way on her own. Max could make it to Hana, get off the island and back to the FBI. At least they would know she was in danger. Max must have someone he could trust at the agency.

"You really are some field agent, Rio."

Her gaze rocketed over his face. It was a telling moment for her. They'd managed this far with someone on their tail, but the thought of separating from him felt like betrayal. She was up to the challenge of playing hide-and-go-seek with Fuentes's men. She was scared for Max, but she shouldn't be. He was an agent. He'd had training just as she'd had, yet so had Shane and he was dead.

"Nothing better happen to you, Max."

Max offered a comforting smile as he captured the back of her head, drawing her nearer. She went eagerly. His mouth covered hers, a brief, hot slide of lips and tongue speared a stab of desire through her, and she clung to him, forgetting the danger and drinking in his kiss. Damn they were good at this, she thought, and she wanted the chance for more—without guns blazing around them and the threat of Fuentes. He drew back, met her gaze, then kissed her again so tenderly it made her throat tighten.

"I can handle myself, Rio. Don't worry."

"I'll worry until we're out of this and we're both safe." She pulled the clothes out of the pack, along with soap and a towel.

"That waterfall will make a nice shower." Max turned to look at the rushing water.

"Do you think we have time for the luxury?" Rio's skin had started to itch from the salt water and the flight through the forest.

"Sure. I think they'll be back full force at early light, but they're not going to crash around in the jungle looking for us in the dark. They have us over a barrel since we're on an island. No way off without using public transportation."

"Let's clean up, then, rest and get going an hour

before dawn." Rio rose and slipped the straps of the dress off her shoulders. Max's eyes focused on her like bright blue beams in the night.

"That's a good plan." He licked his lips and stood. "Need help with your dress?"

"I've been dressing and undressing myself for years, Max. Hmm, ever since I was six or so." Giving him a sly smile, Rio slipped off her dress, revealing the white lace see-through bra and underwear she wore beneath. She bent over to pull off the once pretty, but now ruined white sandals.

"Damn. You're bleeding," he said. When she looked at him, he gestured to her calf.

She looked and saw blood on her leg.

Max was there, opening the kit and applying the alcohol-soaked gauze that stung and made her eyes water. She hissed in a breath and let it out slowly. "Sorry," he said, looking up at her.

His fingers were so gentle and warm that shockingly, she felt her eyes sting.

Max Carpenter shook her foundations. And she didn't know what to do about that. What she did know was Max was the last person she'd ever reveal that to. He already had a way of looking at her, into her, as if he saw far past her defenses, to some other place she was unaccustomed to people reaching. And that was without her letting him in.

She felt a fine trembling begin in her fingers and start to spread. She needed to find a way to deal with him and succeed in the task at hand without either one of them clouding their thinking further. They couldn't afford to drop their guard. Yeah, right. Tell that to the pulsing, demanding ache that blossomed as soon as he latched those laser beam eyes on her. *So move on as if it's business as usual,* she told herself.

Rio reached down into the pack and pulled out a lethal Glock. She cocked the gun, snapping a bullet into the chamber.

"Expecting problems? Like primates?"

"Primates? Do you think there are any around here?"

"The only primate you have to be concerned with, Rio, is me."

"I don't know," she said. "Sounds like monkey business to me."

6

MAX THOUGHT THERE WAS nothing sexier than Rio standing there in her revealing underwear, holding a very powerful weapon.

"You look pretty good right now. Nothing at all like Mary Poppins."

"Hey, don't go looking for any more trouble."

He met her gaze, loving the dare in her eyes. "You've fulfilled one fantasy."

"Me, in my underwear, holding a handgun? This turns you on?" she asked, arching a tapered brow.

"Yeah."

She snorted. "Men. Can't live with them. Can't shoot them."

"Can't you think of something better to do with me—to me—than shoot me?" he asked, sidling up to her.

"You're a bad special agent, Max Carpenter."

"To the bone."

Reaching down, she cupped him through his jeans. "And a nice one it is. Better yet, you know what to do with it."

"You don't have to fire me up." Then he leaned in

and whispered, "I didn't forget how easy it was to slide into you." Rio moaned and he turned her face to his.

His words didn't stop there. "And the way you taste." He trailed his tongue down her throat. Her head dropped back. "Everything," he said darkly and scraped his teeth over her skin, then took her mouth only to find her taking him in the same heavy way.

Her chuckle was sultry, so feminine it slid over his skin like heated satin.

"Let me put the safety on this weapon," she said before setting it and placing the gun on top of her pack.

"Oh, good. You're talking about the gun."

Her hands moved down his chest and closed over the bulge in his jeans. "Oh, is that a gun? Or are you just happy to see me?"

He nipped at the curve of her shoulder, her collarbone, his hand sliding over her waist, holding her tight lace-clad bottom in his hands.

Kneading, he pulled her hips flush with his.

"Max, you feel so good."

"Wait until I'm inside you, pressed to the hilt."

"Ooooh, I like a confident man." Her eyes danced.

She left him no choice and he kissed her again.

Her laughter transformed into a series of soft gasps as she let him take her. He was beyond thinking about what was smart, and what was supremely stupid. He'd wanted her from the moment he saw her. And, right that very moment, she wanted him back. That was all that mattered.

"Waterfall," she managed to say. "We're on borrowed time."

"Not sure I can walk that far," he said. "Or that I'll ever get these wet jeans off."

"I have a knife," she said, a bit breathless.

He looked down into her eyes, his whole body stiffening in erotic tension. The way she looked up at him made his jeans just that much tighter. At this rate, her cutting him out of his jeans was a sacrifice he was willing to make. "You're not helping with talk like that."

"Max…"

His grin was a quick flash. "I shouldn't like it when you say my name like that. But I do." The grin widened when she looked as if she might shoot him.

Instead, she gripped his loud shirt in both fists and dragged him closer to the falls. A tepid mist coated them, sending droplets running down their skin in little rivulets.

He worked her bra off in one effort and Max sighed in appreciation.

"I know what you're thinking. You might as well say it."

He met her gaze. "Nice rack."

She laughed to herself, shaking her head. "I take it you're a rack kind of guy."

"I am. Yes, I am."

"You just going to look?" She brought his hands to her breasts and the instant he cupped her, wild sensations started coiling out of control. She moaned his name, covering his hands as he massaged her breasts. She leaned back, offering herself, and he loved the breathless sound she made when his lips closed over her nipple.

He worried the tight, hard peaks, then took one deep

into his mouth, the hot pull of fire driving a bolt of heat to his groin.

His hands spanned her rib cage, pulled her down to the mossy bank. He slipped off her lacy underwear until she was completely naked like a forest nymph.

"Another erotic fantasy."

"What?" she asked, laughter in her voice. "A naked woman with a nice rack?"

"Yeah. Is that wrong?"

"You are too much." Her mouth played over his, her tongue laving. He mapped the curve of her behind, his stomach flexing when she opened his jeans, working them down with quite an effort. Then she started on the buttons of his shirt. When she got them undone and pushed it open, he dragged her into his arms, his mouth devouring hers until kisses weren't enough.

They'd never be, Max thought, and sampled the underside of her breast, slick with the moisture from the rushing falls, cascading only a few steps from where they lay. His teeth raked her, his lips closing over her nipple again. She arched into him, her fingers sliding into his hair, holding him right there.

"This is so…amazing."

"You are amazing," he whispered, dragging his tongue down the taut line of her stomach. Her hands went to his shoulders, heat rolling off them. He was surprised they didn't make steam.

He met her gaze and felt shattered, and when she reached between them, he stopped her, catching her hands.

"That could go off prematurely," he said with an indrawn breath. "I want to make sure I hit the target first."

"There's more than one target, G-man."

His dark chuckle rumbled through him before he laid his mouth over hers. Something unfamiliar crackled through him. It wasn't instant, it'd been there, waiting—in that place he'd packed away most of himself. But the suspicion and the distrust dissolved. They were in this together and the need to link himself with her when he'd been solitary for so long was like something calling to him. He kissed her and kissed her until the barrier broke, poured like the pounding waterfall behind them.

"Rio," he murmured.

Her answer spoke when her tongue slid into his mouth, when her hips pressed down on his. Max nearly roared, letting go a little more. His hands mapped her contours and she moaned, a delicious sound that nearly tore through his restraint. Maybe playtime was over.

Maybe not.

Her hands smoothed over his skin, and she dragged her tongue across his nipple, and then suckled.

It left him trembling, his back arched, and he gripped her hips, wedging her closer. His hand slid upward, along her ribs, teasing the underside of her breast.

At this point, life was very uncertain for both of them. Max had to admit he exerted a lot of control and he liked that control.

She teased, drawing back and making him chase her, then erotically licked the line of his lips before she pushed her tongue between. A hot, desperate need riddled him down to his heels as she kissed him. He wanted her right now, on the rocks again, and the image made his cock feel like lead.

She pulled away and his gaze rolled down her body, and everything between them seemed to go still. By increments she leaned closer, her nipples grazing his chest. The press of flesh to flesh held a sort of euphoria, crossing the line of intimacy. Max had helped a lot of people, rescued many, took lives to protect the innocent, but nothing compared to this. He fought for patience, his body flexing with need.

He rolled with her and her indrawn breath told him he'd surprised her, but she hung on.

He moved low, across her stomach; carefully he spread her legs, moving between.

He held her gaze as his finger followed the edge where her thigh met her groin. He found her and her gasp tumbled into his mouth as he stroked her. At eye level, he missed nothing—her panting, the way her hips started to move with him or her scent.

"Max, please."

He thrust his fingers inside, and her hips left the ground, but he pushed her back till she lay flat, then his mouth was on her, tongue delving, and Rio moaned softly.

"Oh, Max. Oh dammit."

He flicked her clit, and then circled it, over and over as his fingers slid in and out. He watched her writhe, draw her legs up and thrust her hips. He wanted to be deep inside her, yet Max held her there, a testimony to his restraint when he wanted to slam into her and fuck her silly. But this was different.

She sat up and climaxed in his arms, clinging to him, her hips thrusting, her expression startled and so unlike any before. Transformed in ecstasy. A little wild, a little innocent. And he held her as she rode the wave of pleasure. Max almost came just watching her.

When she settled she went limp, but not for long. She pushed his erection down, the tip throbbing, and Max gripped her hips, dragged her close and slid into her in one smooth stoke. Eyes locked; they both breathed hard. The solid length of him was heavy and warm.

Her nipples barely touched his chest. His fingers drove into her hair, tipped her head back. It was a possessive move, capturing her, and when she rocked, his kiss deepened. His hand slid down to close over her breast, his thumb making lazy circles while his other hand guided her, urged her. She never broke eye contact, her body undulating like the vast ocean against vast shores.

Max glanced down to see himself disappear into her body. He slammed his eyes shut and fought for command, to keep words he probably shouldn't say from spilling out. Though planted deep inside her, his body wasn't listening. He leaned in, kissing, easing her to her back. He withdrew and thrust, and Rio bowed beautifully beneath him. She begged him to come closer, but he'd crush her so he grasped a lip of rock, one hand under her hips, giving them quick motion.

"That's right, Max, faster."

"Rio," he groaned. "I'm trying to hang on."

"Don't. Give it to me."

It broke his control as effectively as an order. Willpower ebbed into a flood of energy and his hips pumped. She responded by taking him in, closing her legs around his hips. She whispered his name, what he was doing to her, how she felt—and her lusty words pushed him to the brink.

Then he felt her tense, quicken, roll her hips in ecstasy as she reached between them to feel him slide deeply into her, then retreat. Her touch was heavy and bold, and he loved this side of her. Her flesh hardened around him, trapped him in a throbbing flex of feminine muscle and slick skin.

Max wanted more, to connect when he hadn't—he wouldn't allow himself to trust. He laced his fingers with hers, trapping her, spread under him like a sacrifice. Hovering on stiff arms, he held her gaze.

"Let go, Max."

His control severed and Max cocked his leg and thrust, driving her across the mossy bed, a primal need taking him over completely. She came and held nothing back from him, whispering her satisfaction. A flex of twisted muscle and slick bodies meshed as his climax joined hers.

Max threw his head back, suspended, the wild grip of her flesh wringing him. Splintered rapture shredded his composure. Yet in the deep throes of release, he noticed things.

Every inch of her skin melded to his, her little tremors, the fear in her smoky eyes. "Aah, Rio, bull's-eye," he said softly, driving his arms around her, the last threads of passion dissolving under a slow, thick kiss.

"That was some nice aim, G-man."

He rolled to his side, gently pulling her injured leg across his, and watched her world come into focus. Her lashes swept up, her eyes soft and satisfied. Her lips curved gently and Max felt air lock in his lungs. Flushed and rosy, she was incredibly beautiful right then.

Needing to touch her again, he brushed her hair back, tucking it in behind her ear.

"You're messing up this timetable, but good, Carpenter."

"Am I? It was worth it."

"We should, you know, get going."

"Okay." But he didn't move.

Rio chuckled. "We have no more time for…"

"This?"

His erection nudged her and he watched her eyes widen. "Max, you sure recover quickly."

"Good reflexes," he replied, giving her a wicked smile. He didn't give her a chance to answer as he took her mouth.

An hour later, they were done with both fooling around and the shower. Working on getting dried off and dressed, Max asked, "You wouldn't happen to have any food in your Poppins bag, would you?"

She nudged him in the ribs. "Men. It's all about appetite."

"Yep, the no fuss–no muss gender."

He leaned down and kissed the spot where her neck curved into her shoulder.

Dressed in khaki walking shorts now, along with a green T-shirt, a sweatshirt tied around her waist, she slipped on a pair of green socks. Not only did the woman pack for any contingency, but she also matched her clothing while she was at it.

She pulled a comb through her hair, scooped it back

and did some crazy wrapping-and-tucking thing until she had a thick wet bun.

She turned toward him. "I have PowerBars and water, so don't get too excited."

If only she had a clue how easily she excited him, she'd run for the hills.

Even with no makeup, and her cheeks a little flushed from her exertions in the waterfall, Max's body leaped to life as though he hadn't just gotten more satisfaction than that in a very long time. He immediately bent down to lace up the boots she'd provided before she caught him staring at her all moony-eyed or something. She'd also given him a navy blue pair of walking shorts, and a baby-blue T-shirt. She'd matched his socks, too. He smiled to himself. "That would be great. I'd appreciate it."

She gave him a cool look and he wasn't exactly sure why she was a bit distant. Maybe now that things had calmed down, she wasn't sure where things stood between them, or where he wanted them to stand. That made two of them.

She handed him a PowerBar and a bottle of water, then settled next to him. Neither of them spoke for several long moments. "It smells like rain in the air, which isn't surprising since we're sitting smack-dab in the middle of a rain forest, but I for one hope it holds off until we can find some shelter. I don't relish getting wet again."

Rio chewed a chunk of bar then swallowed. "I'm with you on that. I don't have any more dry clothes in my pack."

He nodded.

"So, I'm sure your training in the military helped you blow up two enemy boats."

"Marine. Two tours in Iraq when we first went in. When I got out, I applied for Quantico. That kind of training never leaves you."

"You were a marine?"

He gave her a wistful smile. "There is no past tense, Rio. I'm always going to be a marine." He took a swig of water. "I copped a couple of those missiles they were lobbing at us and did a quick demolition. Thought it would distract them and make them regroup before they came after us again. It's at least a ten-mile hike to Hana from here."

Rio sighed. "But they probably have radios or cell phones."

Max paused and thought about that. "Speaking of cells…do you have one on you?"

She shook her head. "No, I purposely left it back at the hotel. They could trace us with the phone."

"No forms of communication in that magic bag of yours?"

She gave him a quelling look.

"What?" he asked, lifting his hands. "I've gotten used to you pulling a rabbit out of your hat."

"Have you? I suppose you think you're funny? Why don't you use your gut instinct to get us out of this mess?"

He grinned, he couldn't help it. "Well, my instincts told me not to get too tangled up with you, and you can see where that landed me." He watched the color steal into her cheeks, but she didn't look away.

"So you're saying you only listen to them when they suit your purposes?" She took a sip of water.

"Or until someone ambushes me with sexy underwear and a big gun."

"I didn't ambush—"

Now it was his turn to give her the quelling look. The blush that flushed her skin was even more becoming this time around.

"Okay, so maybe I did. Just a bit. But it wasn't my plan for us to end up…the way we ended up."

"But…"

She didn't bother pretending. Her grin was as bold as his was. "Okay, but I'm glad it did." She folded her arms in front of her. "So, now what do we do?"

His eyebrows lifted a fraction. "Regarding which event?"

She laughed.

And his heart teetered dangerously inside his chest. "You're going to get us both in trouble, you know that."

"I thought I already had. You're the protector and defender. You're supposed to keep us on the straight and narrow, focused on the mission at hand." She lifted her shoulders and batted her eyelashes at him. "I'm just the helpless female in this scenario, remember?"

He snorted. "There is nothing remotely helpless about you."

"Thank you," she said. Then, in a more serious tone she added, "Most of the time, I'm pretty fearless about going after what I want."

"I'll vouch for that," he said dryly, hoping to bring back that cocky smile.

Her lips curved ever so slightly. "I'll admit that I'm not exactly ready to run up the white flag or call in reinforcements, but the situation here is starting to rattle me." She held his gaze steadily. "I should have been more thankful for your timely intervention."

"You'd have done something about it, taken action, whether I'd shown up or not."

"Probably," she agreed. "But I don't think I'd have put it all together as quickly. And that might prove to be the difference in getting out of here alive."

She was such a paradox. Here she was, admitting she needed him, that she was grateful for his help, the same woman who'd just about undone him…and yet there was still a wariness about her that had him wondering what it was going to take to win her over completely.

Which was insanity. Because winning her over was not the objective here. Solving her problem was the only goal that needed achieving, and when that was accomplished, he'd go home. And she'd go back to work. So there was no point in winning anything. He'd tried to tell her that last night.

And yet, he couldn't manage to find any regret for what had just happened between them. Sure, it wasn't going to end well. Shit happened in life, and some of it was no fun. But being with her was giving him something he'd never had or felt before. Sometimes when shit happened, it was good.

Max finished his bar and his water and wiped his mouth with the back of his hand. "So here's the plan, then. We need to find a place where I can make a phone call."

"Why?"

Rio took his empty bottle and wrapper and slid them into her pack. Smart not to leave any evidence they were here.

"Remember the guy who saved you in Colombia?"

"Right. Drew Miller."

"I told you he's marrying my sister."

"Right."

"He'll lend us a hand and I know I can trust him."

The snap of her voice told him her feelings. "How? Get us tickets on a commercial flight? What good will that do?"

"No, he's a pilot. He can fly here and get us off Maui and back to L.A., where we can try to figure all this out in relative safety."

She rose and paced away from him, scouring the ground to make sure they hadn't left anything behind. "You're going to involve someone else in this?"

"We can trust Drew."

"I don't care whether or not we can trust him. I don't want anyone else at risk. I will figure something out."

He went to her and grabbed her shoulders to turn her gently so she would look at him. "How, Rio? Western Maui is less populated and we're in the middle of this vast forest preserve. There's no one around for miles. There's no way off this island that isn't being guarded by the Ghost's men. We have to get some help from someone else."

"Can't we just steal a boat?"

"That will show up in a police report and if we're caught on open water, it'll all be over."

"Bribe someone to take us."

"Then we're relying on a stranger. I know I can trust Drew."

"I don't like it."

"That's beside the point, Rio. It's the best and only plan we have, short of shooting our way out of here or trusting law enforcement. I'm not keen on that."

"I'm not, either," she agreed. "My luck is shot to hell both here and in Colombia."

"Have you been fooling around with your karma?"

She gave him a startled look as if that question really hit home. "Karma, that bitch."

"It can be," he said, enjoying that combination of wary amusement he saw on her face. He liked that she fought her attraction to him, or at least questioned it. It meant she was taking this seriously. He didn't examine why that part was so important to him. "But we have something on our side that beats out karma."

"We do? Enlighten me."

"Good old-fashioned training and experience."

Rio nodded. "True."

"We get some rest, wake an hour before dawn and then find a phone."

She leaned in to him. "Okay." She paused, sighed and then seemed to pull herself up a little. "We don't do the expected and head for the airport, at least not to try to catch a commercial flight. We'll confuse him."

"Which is the exact state we want him to be in. Doing the unexpected jars the framework, it forces the other players to adjust their planning. It ups the chances that something or someone might slip up, at least enough to give us another piece of the puzzle. It's important we use what leverage we have to our best advantage."

She nodded again, but her gaze was more intent on him.

"What?" he asked, when she continued to regard him in silence.

"Nothing. I just…" She trailed off, lifted a shoulder. "You're so focused in all this, clearly in your comfort zone, very confident and methodical. On the one hand it reassures me, makes me feel like I can trust you."

"You can," he said automatically. "Always."

She nodded right away, and it was almost ridiculous how good that made him feel. "I know that, in ways that aren't necessarily rational or even proven." She held his gaze. "But I do know that."

"Good," he said, trying like hell to keep the situation all about business. This was hard to do when his heart was celebrating what felt like an important milestone in their relationship. A relationship that didn't exist because it had nowhere to go, he reminded himself.

"On the other hand," she went on, "it scares me. I've had a lot of loss in my life, Max." It was the first time he'd seen her look truly vulnerable. "I don't want anything to happen to you."

He wished he could outright guarantee her he would be fine. But he couldn't do that. She trusted him, and that meant telling her the truth, even when it was a truth she didn't want to hear. "I've pledged to keep you safe, Rio. I'll do that no matter what it takes."

She held his gaze, and then nodded. "That's the thing that scares me the most."

7

PRETENDING TO BE the Ghost's lackey, when, in fact, he was the Ghost, sometimes had its drawbacks. Like now when he was questioned every step of the way. Jammer had learned that hiding in plain sight was all about perception. The Ghost had never been caught because he didn't really exist. He was Jammer's fabrication that had effectively thrown off the DEA, FBI, CIA and all the other alphabet-soup agencies who'd put the Ghost on their ten-most-wanted lists.

Jammer stood on the balcony overlooking the Pacific Ocean. The water was a glittering aquamarine. The warm breeze brought with it the smell of the ocean, and he breathed deep.

With quick flicks of his wrist, he toyed with a butterfly switchblade, flipping the razor-thin blades in and out of the handle. The scissoring sound a soft snick.

He could see a woman on the beach with a small girl, digging in the sand. The woman threw her head back and laughed at something the child said and his heart clutched in his chest. Grabbing up the child, the woman hugged her until the child squirmed.

For a fleeting moment, Jammer wondered what it

would be like to have that. Someone who gave a damn. Her name, her presence was always there at the edge of his mind. *Gina.*

Had it only been two weeks ago that he'd last seen Gina lying in the hospital after a rival arms dealer with a personal beef had tried to kill her by running her over? He'd met her in Paris about a month ago. It was still hard to believe that the delicate woman had put together a major buy with what had been a lethal arms dealer.

Because of her accident, the deal they had planned had been finished by her twin sister and the sister looked so much like Gina, she had almost duped him. But he *knew* Gina on such a deep level that a double couldn't fool him.

He'd fallen way too fast and way too hard for Gina and now he doubted he'd ever get her out of his heart or his head. He let her go for the moment and focused on his purpose.

He was here to capture a woman, a DEA agent, and use the knowledge she possessed to get what he needed to complete this job. That's what he'd told Eduardo.

The drug lord had been livid when the woman had escaped. He'd raged around his compound, lashing out at anyone who even uttered a word.

Fuentes was behind him, the beauty of the ocean and Hawaii lost on him. He paced the hotel room like a caged animal waiting for his pound of flesh.

Jammer was finally where he wanted to be, but the woman had upset his very carefully placed apple cart. Now Eduardo wouldn't rest until he had her back. No one, absolutely no one escaped from him, least of all a

DEA agent. The fact that Rio Marshall was a woman made it all the more unacceptable to Eduardo.

Fucking bastard was jeopardizing a thirty-million-dollar deal because of his pride.

Idiot.

Eduardo had more things to worry about than one lone woman, yet that's what the man was focusing on. To expand their drug-trafficking businesses, drug lords often made deals with other factions. Colombia was filled with paramilitary organizations fighting for their own ideals against the government. The organizations quickly realized that selling drugs was an excellent way to fund their wars, which made drug lords the partner of choice.

Eduardo agreed to find a gunrunner who could provide the troops of the Defensores de la Libertad the weapons they needed and in turn the Libertad would protect Fuentes's interests—his laboratories, his members and associates and his trafficking routes. Namely the Gulf of Urabá, through which hundreds of millions of dollars' worth of contraband—arms and drugs in particular—entered and left Colombia each year. Fuentes had found the Ghost, or his associate, anyway—Jammer.

The deal Jammer was putting together would take him where he wanted to go in Fuentes's organization. A deal that included huge shipments of high-powered machine guns, fragmentation grenades and rocket-propelled grenade launchers, which would cement the relationship between Fuentes and the Libertad.

It had come as a shock to him that he'd recognized

the woman the moment he saw her. Shane McMasters, a name out of his past, one that should stay buried in his memory, rose like a specter. He'd been a DEA agent who'd gotten way to close to Eduardo and had paid by losing his life.

Rio Marshall was his stepsister, and Jammer had every intention of getting her out of the mess she was in. He owed it to the man who had been Shane McMasters. He didn't know what she was doing in the jungle, but she'd escaped Fuentes, made him look weak and ineffectual. When Jammer insinuated that Eduardo's ranks had been breached, it made the drug lord even more paranoid than he was already.

"Hijo de puta!" Fuentes yelled into the cell. His rapid-fire Spanish wasn't lost on Jammer. The woman had escaped somewhere in the Ko'olau Forest Preserve along with the FBI agent who was protecting her.

Jammer turned as a red-faced Fuentes threw the BlackBerry across the room, where it exploded against the wall and left a discernible dent.

The ruthless, untouchable drug lord had tantrums like a little girl.

His dark eyes studied Jammer and he sneered. "They lost the whore and her bodyguard. I'm going to rip their hearts out. Six men against one man and woman? These are the elite guards they send me?"

"Calm down, Eduardo. There's no way for them to escape from Maui. We've got men stationed at all the airports and you've taken care of local law enforcement. There's nowhere for them to go. Eventually, they're going to emerge. When they do, we'll have them. If they do escape, you have your own personal rat who can provide you with every move they make. So, there's no need to panic."

A smile spread across Eduardo's face. "*Sí,* I pay him well for information. He's been very valuable." He stepped up to the balcony, but never even glanced at the majestic ocean. "This woman is like a *gato.* She has nine lives."

"Well, in this case, the cat got too curious. You know what they say about cats and curiosity."

"You are sure this woman came to my compound to consort with one of my people—a traitor to my organization?" Eduardo asked.

"I'm sure. A DEA agent shows up at your secret compound? What else could it mean? At the very least, I don't think we should kill her until we've had a chance to find out. With all the plans that are in place, it would be risky."

"The Ghost agrees with this strategy?"

"He was the one who suggested it."

Eduardo nodded and adjusted his Armani suit. "Then we find her."

"And the FBI agent?" Jammer asked.

"He's expendable. Agreed?"

Jammer shrugged. He couldn't save everyone. "Agreed."

RIO WOKE TO THE WARMTH of Max wrapped around her. Her hand on his chest, her head tucked against his shoulder. She'd dreamed of Shane and a day they had at the beach, but the dream had gotten dark and very scary, then Shane had disappeared. It was odd because she'd had the same type of dream on the plane.

Snuggling against Max, she let the images go. It'd been a long time since she'd woken up in a man's arms, a man she was getting way too accustomed to. She lay still, listening to his breathing, and she heard a twig snap. Carefully she unwound from Max and searched the forest. She reached into the pack and pulled out one of the Glocks. She checked the clip and rose, listening intently.

The waterfall behind her made a soft swishing noise that obscured her hearing, so she moved cautiously away from the makeshift camp.

Peering out into the gloom, she could see no movement whatsoever. The hair on the back of her neck bristled. Turning, she ran to where she'd left Max and said softly in his ear, "We've got company."

Max came awake instantly, one of the Glocks in his fist. "Then let's give them a proper welcome."

"No," she murmured. "I don't think they know we're here. Let's just slip away."

Max rose and grabbed the pack out of her hands. "I'll carry it. You locked and loaded?"

"Yes," she said, relinquishing the pack not altogether voluntarily.

It felt strange to admit to herself she was giving up a little of her control. Obviously, if she wanted the pack, he would give it to her. But she found it seemed right to share the burden with him.

They started off pushing between the trees, the ground vegetation dense and dripping with twilight dew.

Suddenly, shadows were all around them and Max pulled her down to the thick vegetation. A light ghosted over them.

They burrowed deeper into the ground cover, sweat beading on her forehead and adrenaline shooting into her system.

"Thorough bastards." His voice was soft in her ear, his breath sending delicious tremors down Rio's spine.

She tipped her head, his lips brushing her ear. "Great, just what we need. Conscientious killers."

"All this to protect the Ghost's identity?"

She squirmed inside knowing the men hunting them weren't the Ghost's. But he was just as involved. Eduardo Fuentes and what could have been the Ghost's henchman were getting pretty chummy in his compound. She again kept quiet, but it cost her. Max had a right to know what he was up against. But chances were they would get off Maui and there wouldn't be a reason she'd have to tell him she'd lied and was undercover to keep him occupied.

She tensed and put her hand on Max's shoulder. Shortly after that, she heard the footsteps. A bright light swept back and forth over the forest. It was so dense where she and Max hid that the light was only a faint glow. The men neared and Rio held her breath.

The situation felt familiar to her, almost natural. She'd spent so much of her time as a DEA agent traversing dangerous parts of forests and jungles. It was as if she'd been born in the trees.

"How do you do that?" he whispered so close to her ear, his warm breath tickled her skin.

"Experience," she whispered back. "I can almost sense them."

She closed her eyes, and smelled the musty earth tossed up with each careful step, just as she could feel Max's heart pounding where her hand rested on his back. In her hand she held her weapon.

The men shone the light at their feet, took a few steps, and then swept the area high and low. They couldn't do both. On the forest floor there wasn't a shred of moonlight, and it was uneven and crisscrossed with exposed roots. It was one advantage. Rio could see boots now, hear the shift of the dirt and pebbles beneath them. They shuffled, the movement of unsure steps.

Rio slipped her finger over the trigger. Five against two weren't good odds. A firefight would bring more to Fuentes's personal army.

And that was why she'd been in Colombia. It had been her job to find out what deal was going down with the Defensores de la Libertad. She'd gotten the dirt on Fuentes and was making her way back to home base when she'd stumbled across his compound. Then the monkey. Reflexively, she looked up into the trees.

Then a radio crackled and she heard a man respond quickly in Spanish. *No, we haven't located them. It's like they vanished.* There was irritation in the caller's voice, but with the distortion, recognition was impossible. *Remember, I want her alive. Kill the man, but bring me the woman.*

She felt Max stiffen at her side and her stomach lurched into her throat. It was her turn to tense, but Max slipped his hand over the one that held the Glock.

The radio crackled again and this time the man's voice was angry. *Call off the search for tonight. We will begin again at dawn.*

Rio didn't expect them to give up. It was just as she suspected. They wanted her alive and they had every intention of killing Max. She couldn't let that happen.

The men paused to discuss the orders and seemed glad of it. Rio breathed a sigh of relief as they melted back into the forest, moving more rapidly away from them.

There was only one thing for her to do and, for a moment, her throat closed. Then her resolve hardened.

She'd have to leave Max.

MAX HAD TO ADMIT TO himself, it was one thing to think people were out gunning for you, but it was another thing to hear it said so blatantly.

It only served to make him madder than hell.

They rose and Max looked toward the mountaintop in the far distance, its highest peak shrouded in mist and glowing in the crescent moonlight.

"Get the map out and let me have it," he said.

Rio complied and Max unfolded it. Crouching down, he used a small penlight to see it. "Fuentes is going to expect us to make for Hana. I say we head toward Makawao. It's a safer bet. We're about halfway between them, so it's a ten-mile trek either way. He'll probably have everything locked down in Hana and it's a bigger risk for us to go there."

Rio nodded, took the map and folded it, stowing it in the pack.

"Now all we have to do is get our bearings." He

identified the North Star and noted from the map that Makawao was situated to the north of the island.

"Don't hurt yourself there, Galileo. Use my GPS," she said.

He turned to find her holding out the device. "Why didn't you tell me you had a GPS?"

She reached up and ran her thumb between his eyes. "I love the way this furrows when you're being serious."

He chuckled. "Do you?"

"Yup," she replied, "and you didn't ask."

He smiled and she smiled back. The air popped with their chemistry. "You're getting back at me for all those Mary Poppins cracks, aren't you?"

"Payback's a bitch."

He opened his mouth to speak, but she held up her hand. "Stop while you're ahead. That's if you ever want to see me in lace and a really big handgun again."

"Been there, done that. Could we go for an assault rifle and fishnet?"

"You're pushing it, Carpenter."

"Yeah, I know." He met her gaze squarely. "So what about the fishnet?"

Max's smile was slow and she joined him. She laughed and pushed at his chest. They walked for another half an hour before Max shone the light long enough to see his surroundings. "We need to climb."

"I can't tell you how much I'm looking forward to that," Rio said dryly.

His legs felt the burn from the strain, and when he stopped she collapsed against a tree.

"We'll rest here until sunup." With his back to the twisted roots of a tree, Max settled down to the ground and patted the space beside him.

"What a relief." She dropped next to him, snuggling up to him and using his chest for a pillow. "Wake me if you need help kicking ass."

She exhaled long and low, and within seconds she was asleep, her hand on his chest. Max disengaged her Glock from her relaxed grip. He stretched his legs out and laid his own weapon at his side, keeping his gaze on the nearest path several yards ahead. He snuggled her more comfortably. It felt good, her compact body resting against his. It had been a while. Max wasn't proactive when it came to relationships. After a succession of dates, he adopted the lone-wolf way of life until fate threw him a bone. It was as much his fault as his job's. Most women couldn't handle the secrecy and the hours, nor understand his real purpose.

Rio's lax hand drifted to his stomach and his muscles immediately contracted. He gently shifted her hand away from ground zero and tried not to remember what it was like to have her touch him. He wondered how long he'd last without tasting her again.

He wondered about her past. She snuggled closer and he thought *two hours to sunrise.* He'd be lucky if he made it. At least the hard-on she gave him would keep him paying attention.

He had to trust her, but not completely. People did weird things when they were threatened. Yet he had every reason to believe her about the Ghost. The threat was quite real.

"Your brow is furrowing. You're thinking too hard again," she said, and it startled him.

He tipped his head to look at her. She never opened her eyes. "How do you know that?"

"I can tell. What is it?"

"Honestly?"

"No, lie to me." Her tone amused him. "Of course honestly."

"I was wondering about your stepbrother," he said.

"How do you know about that?"

"Your file." His tone almost sounded apologetic.

"His name was Shane McMasters. He was a DEA agent killed in the line of duty. He was a very good man, liked the Bears, sharp cheddar cheese and the Rolling Stones. I buried him three years ago."

"I'm sorry."

"So am I," she said softly.

"Get some sleep, Rio."

MAX HEARD A SUCCESSION of thunks and he started awake. The sun was just peeking over the horizon casting a pink glow, but to Max's sleep-gritted eyes, it stabbed like a penetrating spotlight. His body protested when he shifted and opened his eyes.

Rio was standing in the glade and she was throwing knives into a tree, one after the other with a blinding speed that left him a bit breathless.

"Okay, I changed my mind. Fishnet and throwing knives."

"You are pathetic," she said, and walked over to him,

slipping the knives into a sheath she had concealed beneath her shirt.

"Did you get some sleep?"

"Yes, but it was like lying on a rock. You are one ripped guy."

"I thought you liked it hard?"

She tipped her head, smiling. "What are you saying? A hard man is good to find?"

"Isn't he?" He rose and stretched.

She walked up to him and laughed. Placing her hand on his chest, she slowly moved upward to the back of his neck, her fingers pushing into his hair as she pulled him down.

Max went willingly, and when his mouth touched hers, it was all he could do not to devour her whole. She was warm, her mouth soft and playful, as she teasingly took her time, refusing to let him rush it. He loved how Rio was so patient, when she had been so impatient before.

You're falling for her, he thought, and while internal warnings were going off inside his brain, the sudden dark need for her smothered him as he kissed her back. Her response knocked him sideways, and when he ran his hand down her spine and pulled her tighter, he knew he had to stop this before he lost control. With Rio, losing control was getting easier by the hour.

Max drew back, ran his fingers across her lips and heard her breath rushing in her lungs.

"Damn those bad guys," she said, then grasped his hand to look pointedly at the gun he was holding.

"You're a vigilant guy."

"I'm supposed to be protecting you."

"Don't get your knickers in a twist, Max. I'm aware of our situation."

She brushed dirt off her legs, and then reached for the pack. Max tried to intercept her, but this time she shouldered it. "You know I can handle this, Max."

He could hear her unspoken words. *What I can't handle is you.*

He held her gaze, understanding more than he thought. "Okay, you can carry it."

"I wasn't asking for your permission," she muttered as she moved past him and gave him a light shove.

EDUARDO MOVED SWIFTLY, running through underbrush and across the forest floor as if he were bred for it. Maui wasn't much different from the jungles of his boyhood and he'd been like a jackal in that environment. The elite guard followed but were much slower. The American had elected to stay in the hotel, telling Eduardo he was obsessed with the woman.

No whore of a DEA agent was going to get the best of him, especially a woman.

They hadn't done the expected and headed back to Hana, so Eduardo decided he would track them himself. They had done an admirable job of covering their trail, but Eduardo was an expert tracker. He stopped and checked his progress. They were about five hours ahead of him.

His pride drove him.

Spooked prey was dead prey.

IF ONLY SHE COULD prepare herself for what was going to happen. Her head told her to make a clean break of it as soon as possible and go back to working as she always did: solo. Her heart wasn't so clear on the matter.

She tried telling herself what happened back at the waterfall didn't change anything. She had no intention of jeopardizing Max any further.

She was in a Catch-22. She couldn't tell him who the bad guys really were because she had her orders, so she couldn't explain to him what was really going on. For the first time in her career, it really bothered her.

"Rio," Max said impatiently.

She realized she'd been caught up with her own thoughts and hadn't heard him. "What?"

"Look, I'm sorry about the pack. I just wanted to lessen your load. Sue me for being a freaking gentleman."

She kept walking. She didn't want to acknowledge anything about the kind of man Max was. It was already too painful to think about walking away from him. She needed to keep this about the business at hand.

But Max wasn't the kind of man who gave an inch. He grabbed her shoulder and turned her. "Look, I know you're competent. I know you outdo me in the jungle. Hell, you outdo me period."

Damn he was confident in his own masculinity to admit such things to her. She nodded and turned back to the path, but Max snagged her arm again. "Rio…"

His touch was too much right now and she shrugged out of his hold. "We have to get to Makawao."

"I know, but I'm trying to explain to you—"

"I get it, Max." She looked over at him. His clothes were rumpled, his hair a bit of a tousled mess, and he had a hint of beard stubble lightly shadowing his jaw now. She'd seen him all spiffed up in his dark blue suit and power tie—the FBI uniform. She knew how well he cleaned up, but the way he appeared now seemed so real. It hurt her to look at him.

Max held her gaze for a moment too long, a moment that told her he was probably reading every last thought in her mind.

She softened her tone and sighed. "You're sorry. It's okay."

He seemed satisfied with that. It didn't help much that his general geniality was making her feel crabby and unreasonable. When, in reality, she was generally far more like him, grabbing for the joy in life and doing her best to let the rest go.

She couldn't see there being a future in grabbing for him.

Which meant it was time to let him go.

She went to move forward again, but he waylaid her. "Can I ask you one thing?"

She stilled, feeling him so close, knowing it would likely be the last time he was in her personal space like this. She tried not to feel so disappointed about that, to put it in proper perspective, which was that she was fortunate to have experienced any intimacy with him at all. But it proved to be beyond her compartmentalizing capabilities. She'd get past it in time.

"Ask," she directed him, reaching for what she liked to term her kick-ass voice.

Her skin prickled at his nearness. She purposely kept her eyes on the trail.

"You're not going to skip out on me, are you?"

She jerked her eyes to his and swallowed her words. Taking a calming breath, she lied to his face. "No. We're in this together, like you said."

8

"WHAT ARE YOU DOING?" Rio asked when Max focused on the ground intently for the second time in twenty minutes and then very carefully re-planted his feet into his footsteps.

"Laying a good false trail. Follow my lead. We're going to double back in a bit. I don't trust the Ghost not to have planned ahead. As a marine, I know how to lay a trail even the Shadow Wolves couldn't follow."

"Shadow Wolves?"

"They're this group of Native American trackers who work for the government," he explained as she followed him and tried to place her feet in her previous footsteps.

"What makes you think you can fool these Shadow Wolves?" she asked, eyeing him and the ground.

"They're the ones who taught me to lay the trail. Gave me some of their secrets."

"Like?"

"Make a false trail logical. Don't set it to go off in a direction that doesn't make sense to whoever is chasing you."

"The fact remains though, they have to know we're

headed to an airport. It's the fastest and most logical way off the island."

"Got that. It'll buy us time." He grinned. "What they don't know is we have our own personal pilot. We'll just have to lie low until I can contact him and get him here." Max looked at the sky. "It's going to be dark soon. We should start scouting for a place to lie low for the night."

"After we lay this false trail?"

"I've been setting them all day when we took our rest breaks to eat and drink. You've been preoccupied."

Her expression shuttered completely then, which only made him want to press harder. His gut was telling him there was something definitely wrong here.

"It's okay, you know," he added with complete honesty. "You don't have to pretend otherwise. You'd be foolish not to be worried, and you're anything but foolish."

There was a slight flicker in her expression at his description of her inattention, but he couldn't decipher what it meant.

"You are worried, right?" Max asked, crouching again and then looking up at her.

"Yes, any smart agent would be worried. We're in a high-stress, potentially fatal situation."

"I think it might be a bit more than that."

She rose. Her expression was unreadable now, her gaze steady, but definitely wary.

"We're wasting valuable time," she said.

"Rio—"

"Max," she mimicked. "We need to focus on finding Makawao and getting the hell away from here."

"Mmm-hmm," he said and held her gaze. "I'm not going to stop pushing. You know that."

Her shoulders dropped ever so slightly. And he thought he heard the softest of sighs. "I know."

He pressed a finger under her chin and turned her face gently to his. He smiled, but he was serious. "Why don't you just tell me? If you're worried about my safety, I'd say I'm already committed. I can take care of myself." He drew his fingertips up to her cheekbone and stroked her jawline, "There's no shame in admitting you need me." He caressed her cheek, lowered his mouth to hers. "But I can't do anything unless you let me in." He brushed a soft kiss across her lips. "Let me in, Rio."

She sighed into him, accepted his kiss and then returned an impossibly sweet one of her own. His heart dipped, and then squeezed tightly.

"You're further in than you know," she said briefly rubbing the backs of her fingers over his face. "As in as I can let you." She stroked her thumb over his lips and looked into his eyes. "And trust your own instincts. They're not going to let you down, Max." And then she dropped her hand and ducked her head, removing herself from his touch, if not his personal space. "Now please, we need to figure out where to spend the night. Let's get going."

Max stared at her lowered head for a long, silent moment. She didn't give much, but she asked for even less. So when she did, he listened. She hadn't asked for his trust, but he'd given it.

He understood trust was about more than believing she wouldn't betray him. But it didn't make him feel any less conflicted. He wasn't used to feeling so proprietary or worrying so much about anyone, except his own family.

He swore softly to himself. Partnerships could be tricky at times. He knew that from working with others at the FBI, discovering their boundaries and limits, as well as developing trust and faith. But with Rio there was the added emotional element, which was as huge as it was confusing. That was the part that wasn't rational or reasonable, more like a primal directive to protect and defend. He snorted at himself. Sexist.

Now he had even more questions. And fewer answers. It was driving him insane. She was driving him insane.

"Why couldn't I do something easy?" he muttered. "Like fall for a terrorist."

She reflexively glanced up at him, then immediately looked away. Given she was no terrorist, he could only guess it had been the part about falling.

"I know that unnerves you, but it's there anyway. You'll have to find a way to deal with it, Rio," he said, wanting to shake her. Wanting to take her. Wanting…everything. "You're going to have to find a way to deal with me."

"I'm working on it," she said softly.

"Son of a bitch," Eduardo swore as he looked around the lush, vast valley. Two of his elite guards had caught up with him and they now flanked him. "Those agents aren't pushovers." One of them knew how to lay false trails. He'd been chasing his tail for an hour.

Eduardo raised his head like a dog scenting the breeze and then he saw it. The telltale sign of which way they went. His wolfish grin spread across his face.

Almost howling with glee he set off again, setting a grueling pace. The two men followed.

RIO THOUGHT SHE'D HAD A monkey on her back when that howler had jumped her in Colombia, but it was nothing compared to the two she had on her back right now. One: Max was falling for her. The thought brought her a sliver of joy, but she forcefully tamped it down. Two: she was lying about more than just the Ghost. She was lying about not leaving. That was a really big monkey. So, monkey number two would take care of monkey number one. She could only hope, for his sake, that as soon as he discovered her gone, he would head for Makawao and call his friend. Then he'd go back to L.A. It may be true that Eduardo knew who he was, but that wouldn't do Eduardo any good. The mole would confirm that Max didn't know anything about Colombia.

The only question was: what would she do?

They'd found an idyllic spot to settle for the night. It was a protective and well-hidden pool that afforded a view of the valley spread below them.

It was a strategic location that offered a good vantage point to see anyone approach. She intended to wait until Max fell asleep. She'd take what she needed and leave the rest for him. Some money, the GPS and one of the weapons would do for now. Then she'd get herself off Maui and find her boss and hope he could rectify the situation.

As plans went, it wasn't the greatest, but it would have to do. She'd occupied Max's time as best she could and, if she knew Max, he would be too distracted by what had happened here to immediately go after the Ghost.

The bottom line was that Max would be as safe as she could make him. She knew Fuentes would kill Max if he found him, but the drug lord's focus was on her, not Max. Eduardo was a ruthless man and anyone found with her would be gunned down without question. She couldn't handle losing Max that way. Better that he hate her, but still be alive.

She heard someone approaching and cursed her inattentiveness. When Max emerged from the trees, his arms laden with bananas and a mango, Rio relaxed.

"Where did you get those?"

"Picked them off the trees. Man, this is a beautiful island. It's too bad we're running for our lives."

He looked so proud of himself her heart slammed into her chest. It hurt. Physically. "Yeah, too bad this didn't turn out to be that piece-of-cake assignment you'd hoped for."

"That's for sure. We could have been sunning and swimming for two damn weeks on the government's dime. But then some gunrunner has to come along and screw it all up. Jerk."

She laughed because he was trying to be funny and he expected her to be amused. Inside she was anything but. Max was turning out to be someone she could see herself with for the rest of her life.

Too bad she was too afraid of losing someone to risk it. Alone was the way to be.

If she didn't feel for anyone, then she wouldn't hurt so bad when they were gone. It seemed so logical when she thought of it. Now, it seemed like self-preservation.

"Let me have one of those sharp knives."

"You know, Chef Carpenter, those knives are not for carving up fruit. I need them pointy and sharp."

"I don't know about you, but I haven't eaten mango straight from the tree. I bet it's succulent and juicy. Can you sacrifice some of your sharpness for a little sweet?"

She pulled one of the knives out of its sheath and handed it to him. "Be careful, it's really sharp."

Max smiled. "When we get out of this, I'll cook you a real meal. What do you think about that?"

Her heart turned over. "I think that would be amazing."

"That's right. It'll taste amazing."

"That's not what I'm talking about. The fact that you cook is amazing."

"Hey," he said, "you can judge me after you've tried my meatballs with orzo. My sisters love it."

"Well, they're family," she said dryly.

He got her around the neck in a headlock and wouldn't let go until she yelled uncle. Then they ate the delicious mango and bananas, washing the fruit down with one of the two bottles of water they had left.

"So, was your brother one of those fun brothers or did he find his little sister to be a nuisance?"

Rio's insides knotted up. Shane had been the perfect brother. "He taught me how to catch a baseball and how to slide into home base. He took me to the movies and bought me popcorn." She paused as the memories of her brother washed over her. "He helped me with my homework," she finished hoarsely.

"So, he's a good guy."

"Was."

"What?"

"He was a DEA agent and he was killed in the line of duty."

"I'm sorry about that, Rio."

"It was three years ago."

"That must have been so hard. Losing your mother and father and then your brother."

"It was. It was extremely hard for me." What she hadn't expected was that her stepbrother would die and leave her with such rage.

It was all due to one man.

Eduardo Fuentes. Her need to see him convicted for all his crimes, not just her stepbrother's murder, was a relentless force that drove her.

Max went to the pool and washed his hands off, drying them on his shorts. The sun was setting and Max seemed to glow in the fading light. He looked up and Rio was struck by not just the physical attraction she had for Max's dark good looks, his hard-muscled body, but for the man he was, as well. A man with integrity. He wouldn't easily tolerate liars.

She was banking on it.

He walked back and sat down. "It's a beautiful sunset. Come sit next to me and we can both enjoy it."

"Someday I'll have to come back here when I can enjoy it and not worry about bad things and bad people," she said. A sigh escaped her lips when Max put his arm around her and shifted her to his lap.

"Mmm. I think I have a better view," he said as he trailed his mouth down the side of her neck. "Much more interesting to me."

"*You* are going to miss this spectacular sunset, Max." She laughed and his arms came around her waist. In a move that she couldn't control, she arched against him.

"You know," Max murmured just beneath her ear, "we could say to hell with all this, find a hotel with our wad of cash and stay for a few days." He nipped her earlobe. "Weeks." He tightened his arms around her waist and snuggled her against the growing bulge in his shorts. "Maybe a month would do it. Maybe."

"Maybe," she repeated a bit breathlessly as his palms flattened on her stomach and started to slide upward. She was trying like hell to keep her gaze focused, if somewhat unsteadily, on the valley below. But Max wasn't making it easy.

Nor was she scrambling to get off his lap.

He cupped her breasts, gently catching her nipples between his fingers as he squeezed. A moan slipped out as she arched into his hands, and any thought of the valley and her all-important mission dimmed substantially.

"Max—"

"Shh, it's all about the sunset."

No, she thought, it was all about Max. And she wanted more of him on her. He nibbled at her nape, making her shudder, then slid one hand down between her legs, undoing a button or two to allow him to slide his fingers along the inside of her thigh.

"We…should—"

"Do more of this," Max murmured roughly. "Come for me, Rio." He stroked the cotton panel between her legs as he continued toying with her nipples and nibbling her neck. She was going to stop him and focus on the job, really she was. But she was tired, and hungry, and needy as all hell, and this felt way too damn good to stop. So she let her eyes drift shut, let the sensations take over, let Max take over, and promised herself she'd regain control the moment it was over. Promised herself she'd come to terms with Max and his effect on her.

Just as soon as he made her climax. Again.

She was still shuddering, still jerking against his hand and the oh-so-clever fingers he'd slid inside her, when he was already slipping them out and shifting her around so she faced him. He took her mouth with his, even as he whisked his hand between them to unbuckle and unzip. "Let me in," he breathed against her lips.

And she could have told herself it was only fair to let him have his, since he'd so thoroughly seen to hers, but the raw truth of it was she was craving the feel of him, filling her up, as she'd never craved anything before. She would have pushed his hands away and torn at his shorts herself if she'd thought it would get him inside her any faster.

She was pushing at her shorts and he was tugging at his, and they'd barely freed what had to be bared when he was jerking her down on top of him. She pushed down as hard as she could, grinding on him, glorying in the long groan of satisfaction she wrenched from him as she rode him until every last spark of need was sated to its fullest extent.

His hands were on her hips, his mouth on hers, his tongue deep inside. Just as he was thrusting, she matched him. She took both as fast and deep as she could. She felt him gather beneath her as his own climax built. She bit his bottom lip, making him growl and buck higher, which made her cry out as he reached a place even deeper inside her. She tightened her fingers in his thick black hair and held on as his fingers sank into the soft flesh of her backside, likely marking her there as he tugged her harder, faster, against his now-bucking hips.

He reached some spot that sent sparks shooting all over again, and she arched back, trying to keep him right there, on that spot. And her arching took him over the edge, groaning, growling, as he pistoned inside her while coming in a shuddering fury.

She clung to him when it was over, and he clung just as tightly to her, clutching her to him, even as she struggled to stay upright in his lap, her fingers still in his hair, her face buried in the crook of his neck.

Their breaths came in heavy pants, and she slowly became aware that she was damp and sweaty. The air was heavy with the smell of rain.

She reeled from the need to keep this man safe. Joining this way with him was more than she'd ever felt for any other man. It was a special kind of love that lasted a lifetime, but she knew that she couldn't take what he offered. Her heart simply broke inside her at the thought of leaving him, but she had no choice. She was going to lead Eduardo's goons off if it was the last thing she ever did.

It was shocking to her that she and Max had found each other in the midst of this dangerous situation. Of course, the suspense certainly heightened their sensations, so there was that element, as well, feeding into this.

None of which explained the knot in her stomach, or her reluctance to let him go, to look him in the eye and share this wonderful thing, and then place it out of bounds. Did she have the courage to walk away and not look back?

Max's tight grip was crushing, but she understood it. He wasn't ready to let her go, either. His arms tightened around her reflexively when she tried to move away.

But she willed herself to break contact, sever the bonds that made her too weak.

She would have pulled away, but he pressed his lips against the damp, heated skin of her neck, the kiss sweet and gentle. She almost lost it there, but instead kissed him, drawing her mouth closer to the hard edge of his jaw, before nuzzling against his cheek, until he turned his face and met her lips with his own.

They kissed, softly, silently, reverently. Every moment of which quenched her thirst for him in a way that the most fierce, rocking orgasms could never hope to match.

"We should get back on guard."

"Yes," Max said, his voice raspy and sounding gruff.

She did move then, but he captured her face between his palms before she could slide completely off his lap. His expression was as serious as she'd ever seen it, his gaze locked on to hers so intently it was as deep a connection as the kisses they'd just shared. There was a stunned silence between them, the power of which she saw reflected in his gaze, as well.

It was both a relief to know she wasn't alone in reeling from the magnitude of what she'd felt had happened just now, even if she couldn't define it, as well as a threat to what little sense of self she still maintained.

She had no idea what would happen now, what meaning he might draw from this, or what actions it might motivate him to take. Those thoughts both alarmed and thrilled her.

He said nothing, just held her gaze for the longest moment. Then he took her hand and pulled it up to his mouth. He nipped each fingertip, and then kissed them each, too. Then he closed his eyes and kissed the center of her palm before curling her fingers—still damp from his mouth—over it.

He wrapped his hand around hers as he looked up into her eyes, his own an almost impossible cerulean blue now through the thick fringe of his dark lashes. "I trust you. I trust us. That's a promise. Don't lose it. Keep it safe."

She was torn by the almost overwhelming instinct she felt to pull his hand up and give him the same gift, demand the same vow, startled by how strong the urge was to bind herself to him in such a significant way. Ultimately…she couldn't. There was so much between them, but even more still left unsaid. And if she couldn't tell him the rest, then she had no business making promises. Of any kind.

And yet she curled her fingers tightly into her palm knowing he felt her do it. It was as much of a vow as she could make. That she did, indeed, want what he wanted. She just couldn't accept making such a promise.

She couldn't keep it safe.

Not without putting at risk the trust that had already been bestowed on her, and the vows she'd made to her dead stepbrother, her agency and the boss she so respected.

SHE LAY NEXT TO HIM on the soft bed he'd made of leaves, waiting for her chance. She sighed heavily, quite disgusted with her pent-up self, and tucked her arm beneath her head. She was staring at the sky, but seeing something else entirely. Someone, actually.

Max Carpenter.

He was the most confounding man she'd ever met.

Mostly because he'd given his trust to her so deeply and she was only minutes away from breaking it completely.

Maybe that was why she was stalling.

She rolled to her side, agitated, too sick at heart to be closer to him. The warmth of him drew her, but she had to do this. It was the only way to keep him safe and to break her tie with him.

The moon was a big, round ball of light in the sky and she closed her eyes against the pain. She was glad she'd had those last moments of closeness with him. It would have to last her a long time.

A lifetime.

Okay, she had to stop procrastinating. She rose up on her elbow, waiting a moment for her eyes to adjust to the darkness a bit more.

Max slept on his side, one arm close to his body, but the other extended as if reaching for her.

She looked away and rose. Silently she made her way

over to the backpack and took the items she needed. He'd have no problem finding Makawao.

It was dead ahead of them, but she needed the GPS to get her farther away from here, drawing off Fuentes's attack dogs.

She silently moved out of the camp and down into the valley, until she got to Max's false trail. It would be the most logical place for Fuentes's men to spot her. She made sure of it. She brought up the GPS and then consulted the map. She'd head to Pukalani.

From there she could rent a car and somehow charter a flight, or contact her boss. Max had been right. She'd either have to trust a stranger or put other people at risk. She wasn't without skills, but stealing a boat wasn't a good idea.

"Our lives are so very different, Max," she said, her voice not much more than a hushed whisper. She lifted her gaze to where he was sleeping and her heart felt crushed in her chest. "Goodbye."

She turned toward the west, consulting the GPS one more time. Tucking it into her pocket, she took off at a run into the dark night.

Alone.

Just as she liked it.

She'd draw the wolves off Max, and set them squarely where they needed to be. Right on her heels.

Whatever happened over the next few hours, she'd already resolved one thing: pairing up with Max wouldn't have worked. She was doing her thing solo. It was pure fantasy to have believed, even for that one shining split second, that there was ever going to be another way.

9

It was still dark when Rio hit the outskirts of Pukalani. She started seeing signs of civilization. She also knew she was being followed. She put on more speed, but the fatigue was catching up to her. Her heavy breathing could attest to that.

She used the gently sloping terrain to her advantage, adapting to the topography of Maui as easily as she would if she were in Colombia, or Fiji, or New York.

Rio hurried as fast as she could in the dark, skidding down a slope, then feeling it rise again. At the next dip, she changed direction. Ducking behind the curve of the hillside, she waited. Only one man came over the hill after her.

She reached for the weapon she'd placed at the small of her back. When her hand settled over the grip, someone grabbed her wrist, spun her around and hit her hard in the chest so that she fell to her back.

She gazed into the eyes of Eduardo Fuentes and fury ignited in her, burning hotter than a blue flame. Before he could utter a sound, she was up and at him, her fists and feet flying. It was clear he was used to bodyguards because it took him too long to react and Rio laid him out cold.

She bent down to pick up her Glock, thinking one shot to his head and it would all be over. But that decision was taken out of her hands.

Another man came over the rise and she instantly recognized him. *Max.* What was he doing? He was completely out in the open and vulnerable. But before she could do anything, the crack of a rifle reverberated in the night and she saw Max clutch his arm and dive for cover.

Rage and pain gripped her as she saw a man rise and his intent was clear.

Rio raced toward him, but he rolled to his side and fired. Bullets chipped the ground near her thigh and she flung herself to the ground, losing her gun. The thug approached, but Rio leaped to her feet and balled up her fist, hitting the man as hard as she could. He staggered back and dropped his rifle. Snatching up the weapon, Rio cracking the butt of the gun against the man's temple, driving bone into his brain.

Max rushed to a stop in time to see it.

The man dropped instantly, but he wasn't dead, his body convulsing. Rio staggered, her gaze locked on the man's bloody head.

Max walked over to her, his eyes full of anger and relief, cocked the Glock and finished off the goon.

His arm was bleeding. But he offered her his hand to help her stand. "Max, I'm—"

"Can it, Rio," he growled. "We don't have time for that now. There's a pick-up truck not far from here. Let's go. I've got a feeling the Ghost isn't done yet."

She bit her tongue. Now was not the time to say

anything about who was really after her. Eduardo was unconscious and so close, only a jog away. She could go back and just finish him off. But Max was bleeding from a wound in his arm and she'd need to administer first aid. Max was simply much more important. There was also no way of knowing how many other goons they had on their trail.

Max led the way to the truck that was parked next to a grove of pineapples; the trees were planted in neat spiral rows that looked like the whorl of a fingerprint.

"Get in," he said. "You'll have to drive."

He never even asked her if she could hot-wire the truck, and after a minute, she got it started.

Max didn't say a word, but she could feel the anger and sense of betrayal that emanated off him. She had been trying to get away from him to keep him out of danger. True to form, he couldn't seem to let her go.

When she saw the sign for the vet clinic, she pulled off the road. Max had fallen asleep by then and it didn't take long to break in to the clinic to steal what she needed. To assuage her feelings of guilt, she left cash on the counter to pay for what she'd taken.

She cleaned Max's wound and gave him a few stitches. She headed toward Pukalani and found a place to ditch the truck. After using an untraceable credit card to pay for the car rental, they were back on the highway.

"We're headed away from the airport," Max said.

"Yeah, we need to find a safe place to call your friend and get some sleep. They won't expect us to head in the wrong direction. We'll go to Wailea and find a hotel. I want a shower and some clean clothes."

Every bone in her body ached, half-healed cuts and bruises in turn painful and stinging. Her feet throbbed in her boots and it would be good to have a chance to take them off and get some sleep in a real bed. She was done with roughing it for now.

He refused to look at her and she had to understand why, but it still hurt. With the loss of blood, the pain-killer and antibiotics he received, Max fell asleep again.

It was a relief. The guilt twisted her up inside, but it was nothing compared to how she felt when she saw that man pointing a gun at him. Max could be dead now and it would be all her fault. She made the decision to separate from him and she still thought it was a better plan than sticking together.

"Why couldn't you have just left me," she murmured.

She wanted him to go on his own, and the only way to do that would be to tell him something that would show she wasn't worth all the energy he put into protecting her. She had lied to him and soon he would find out to what extent.

It would violate the strict edict her boss had given her, but, at this point, she didn't care. He shouldn't have given her the assignment in the first place.

Suddenly, she wondered why he had. She'd been injured, not at the top of her game. Her suspicious mind grabbed on to the most logical reason. Her boss was trying to keep her out of the way, too. With her and Max ensconced in a cozy getaway for two, her boss effectively killed two birds with one stone.

The man she'd seen at Fuentes's compound.

It had to be that. It had to be. She knew him from somewhere and her boss didn't want her to remember where. It begged the question: why didn't her boss want her to remember where she'd seen the man in Fuentes's compound? What was the DEA trying to hide from her?

That added another layer to this already crazy situation she and Max were in. It was time to leave Maui and ask some pointed questions. In the meantime, she'd have to work on the dilemma of exactly who that man in the shadows was.

RIO SAUNTERED INTO THE hotel like a regal queen, not someone who was covered in dirt and grime, and a little blood. She gave them a good story about their car going off the road and how they'd lost all their luggage.

When she went to pay with a credit card, Max grabbed her wrist, ignoring the pain in his arm that pounded in time to his heartbeat. Even with the sleep he'd had, fatigue dragged on him.

"It's okay, sweetie," she said. "I'll pay."

When she finished the registration and they walked away from the desk, he asked, "Do you think that was smart?"

"It's a card I applied for under my deceased aunt's name. I signed up for it right after I went into the DEA. I only use it in emergency situations."

"That's handy and also illegal."

"I know. But I'm not defrauding anyone. I pay the bills."

Max had to cut her some slack. She used the card to support her job working for Uncle Sam. What could he say? He'd been involved in stealing a truck and medical supplies from a vet.

Max had to give her credit, and he gave it grudgingly because he was still stinging from her duplicity. This was why he didn't trust easily. He knew by the way she'd been acting she had plans to run. He wasn't asleep when she stole out of camp, and it was only a matter of minutes before the men who'd been following them had shown up. It was an easy task to find her trail since she'd mucked with his carefully set false ones. When they set off after her, he followed.

A part of him was deeply relieved to know his instincts had been right all along. And yet, another part of him still felt thoroughly betrayed she'd held back when he hadn't. This made no sense, since he'd pressed her about whether she was hiding something.

He had this gut feeling if he let her out of his sight, he'd never see her again. And trust had nothing to do with it. Things were happening here, things he didn't understand. Until he had a better handle on who the players were and what the stakes were, he didn't really want to separate from her.

He could see the fatigue etched on her face quite clearly now, and knew he didn't look much better. "Let's get a hot shower and hot food."

"No," Rio corrected him as she headed for the boutiques. "We need some clothes. Once I take these off, I don't want to have to put them on again."

He understood that reasoning quite clearly.

"You go up to the room and shower. I'll be up shortly."

"I think it's better if we stick together."

She looked at him with sorrow in her eyes, but nodded.

What could he say? She had to know he wasn't going to be as gullible as he'd been in the forest when he thought they had been working together only to find out she'd lied right to his face. He just had to wonder how long she'd been stringing him along.

He stared after her as she disappeared among the racks of clothing and felt his heart twist in his chest.

THIRTY MINUTES LATER MAX stepped out of the hottest shower he'd taken in a long time, happy to be clean, but not feeling as rejuvenated as he'd hoped. He knew that part of that was the betrayal he tried to get over, quite unsuccessfully. Rio hadn't come into the bathroom, but maybe she had stayed away for fear of his rejection. He really didn't want to make up right now. He needed to think and she would be a distraction.

Max was already confused enough. And he was feeling more preoccupied having been through the emotional roller coaster of the past several hours. Falling in love was a bitch.

Then he stepped into the master suite and found Rio stretched out on the bed, fast asleep. He admitted that falling in love was also one of the best feelings in the whole world. The relief was far greater than it probably should have been, but he was human. She'd stayed. And she was okay. In some ways, on some levels, that was all that mattered to him right now.

His body behaved in a predictable male way upon seeing her all flushed and relaxed, her dark auburn lashes stark against her cheeks. But this swelling sen-

sation was new to his heart and would take him a while
to absorb fully.

He hated to wake her, but he knew she wanted to be
clean. She'd said so in the car. He was struck by how
little he really knew her. And by how badly he wanted
to change that.

Even now his anger was abating. He could understand why she ran. She was trying to protect him, but
if he hadn't come along when he did, who knew what
would have happened?

He rubbed the towel over his hair, but paid far more
attention to her sleeping form than to the new clothes
tucked away in the colorful shopping bags she had
dropped near the bed. He'd never seen power shopping,
but Rio had been a whirlwind of activity in the store
while he waited and kept a keen eye out for anyone who
looked remotely suspicious.

He shook his head. Champion field agent, siren and
martial arts expert. It seemed she was also quite the
champion shopper, too.

"Are you still mad at me?" she asked, her voice soft
and drowsy with sleep.

He glanced up at her in time to watch her stretch. He
was supremely content to have a front-row seat to that
beautiful spectacle. The arching alone was well worth
the price of admission. Even though his body once
again took on the predictable male role, his emotions
were far too turbulent to deal with the temptation, so he
turned and sat on the bed, rummaging through the bags.
"Did they teach you power shopping at Quantico? I
must have missed that class."

"It was an elective."

He glanced over his shoulder.

Her cheeks were a little rosy with sleep, her hair softly tangled around her face, her eyes a bit unfocused. "Did you guess at my size?" he asked. "I hope this stuff fits. Now that I'm clean, I don't want to put on those dirty clothes."

"I had my reasons, Max." The serious look on her face was as provocative as her smile. She sorely tested his willpower.

"What were you thinking? We're stronger together."

"I didn't want you involved anymore. They were going to kill you on sight."

"You were trying to protect me."

"Yes, as crazy as that sounds, I was. I couldn't bear having your being hurt or worse on my conscience, Max."

"If they caught you, Rio, they'd kill you as soon as they got the information they wanted."

"I didn't intend to get caught. I was sure that I could make it to Pukalani and a rental car."

"Then what?"

"I would have thought of something. I'm not without skills."

Thinking about her skills was not a good use of his time right now. *Keep your cool, Carpenter.* Time was ticking again.

He searched through the bag closest to him, but immediately set it aside when his fingers hooked a scrap of black lace. His body had enough to work with without sexy props. In the bag next to it, he found briefs and socks that looked to be his size. Checking out the last bag netted him T-shirts, one green and the other gold. He chanced looking at her again. She'd sat up now, her legs relaxing against the side of the bed. "So, underwear, socks and shirts. I'll take it, but eventually, I want to leave the room." It was a joke, but since she didn't know him that well, he added, "I can make do with the ones I was wearing."

She leaned over and snagged the bag with the black thong in it and pulled out two pairs of shorts. "I gave you a choice, khaki or black. They took your boots for cleaning when you were in the shower."

He looked at her and sighed. "Are we okay for now?"

"There's more."

"I'm not going to like this, either, am I?"

She scooped up two bags and skipped by him on her way to the shower.

"No. You're not. You think you're pissed now."

It took almost superhuman control not to reach out and snare her and her bags full of lacy things and throw them all on the bed. Instead, he grabbed a pair of boxers.

She slipped into the bathroom and closed the door between them.

He looked down at the briefs and shrugged. He wasn't going to push her, but it was good to know she was finally going to open up to him. He just wondered what it was she had to tell him.

He heard the shower go on and tried to block the mental images that came with what would be a provocative sound. "Right." Disgusted with his inability to get his head back on straight—and leave the other one out of it—he tugged on socks and a T-shirt in record time, then checked out the shorts. It was a necessity, a favor. And yet thinking about her purchasing these items for him felt stupidly personal. Intimate even. "You are so gone," he muttered.

He finished dressing, raked fingers through his drying hair and rubbed a hand across his chin, silently thanking her for thinking of purchasing a disposable razor. He tossed his old clothes into one of the empty bags, then after another lingering look at the bathroom door, stalked out into the main room of the suite and used a throwaway phone they'd picked up in the hotel.

Drew answered on the second ring. "Miller."

"Drew, it's Max. I need your help."

"What's up?"

"I've gotten myself into a bit of a bind."

"We were wondering. You were supposed to have dinner with us last night. We suspected it was FBI stuff, but Allie was worried."

"I didn't mean to worry her. I was going to call a couple of days ago, but things went from bad to worse."

"Tell me what you need. We can deploy immediately."

"I need a helicopter to get us back to L.A."

"Check. Where are you?"

"Maui."

"Come again?"

"Maui."

"In Hawaii?"

"Yes. It's a long story."

"I can't wait to hear it. Where in Maui do you want egress?"

"Kahului Airport. How long before you can get here?"

"Give me eight hours to get there and get what I need. Is it just you?"

"No. I have someone with me."

"Is this person hot?"

"Yes, as a matter of fact, you know her."

"Her. Now I really can't wait to hear. Spill it."

"Rio Marshall."

"What? Didn't I just pull her ass out of Colombia two weeks ago…? Hang on. Don't tell me you have a Colombian drug lord on your tail?"

"I don't know if it's a drug lord, but the Ghost is involved."

"That fucking bastard is everywhere."

"I know. Get here as fast as you can and, Drew…bring some firepower with you."

"Will do. Lie low and I'll call you when I touch down."

"Drew, thanks."

"Don't mention it. I'm marrying your sister and you're family. If you can't trust your family, who can you trust?"

THE HELICOPTER LANDED AND Jammer got out of the bird. He walked over to Eduardo, who was pacing again and swearing a blue streak.

He turned on Jammer when he saw him. "You. You're the one who convinced me to take this woman alive."

"What? She clocked you?"

"She got the jump on me." He held a cloth to his cheekbone and Jammer could see the man was going to have one hell of a shiner. This wasn't good for that little DEA agent. But he couldn't abandon her.

"I still want her alive and if you want all the weapons that I've amassed for the Libertad, you had better make sure that's the way she comes to me."

"This is a threat?"

"No, it's a request, Eduardo. The Ghost is prepared to supply all the weapons you need. We won't tolerate a loose cannon out there. So let's think about their next step."

"Obviously, she'll head to an airport."

"We've got all of them staked out."

"Good, we'll get her there."

Jammer walked back to the waiting helicopter feeling the tension between his shoulder blades. He had to make sure Eduardo forgot about the woman and got his mind back on the matter at hand. The whole deal he'd been working on could blow up in his face if he didn't play this scenario the right way.

RIO RINSED THE SHAMPOO from her hair and tried to keep her anxiety down to a minimum. When Max found out about who was really after her and why they were really in Maui, he was going to be so angry.

That suited her plan, right? He would hopefully want nothing to do with her and get out of the line of fire.

Max was too smart not to sense there had been something wrong with her. It hurt that he hadn't trusted her to do the shopping alone. Losing his trust would be something she'd regret probably for the rest of her life.

She finished rinsing off and stepped out of the

shower, only to be assaulted by the heady fragrance of freshly prepared food. Even the smell of coffee had her stomach grumbling. She shoved aside her concerns about the situation with Max and quickly dressed. She ran a fast comb through her hair.

She stepped out of the bathroom to find the bedroom empty, but she could hear Max talking in the main room of the suite. She wasn't sure which was more enticing, the sound of his deep voice, murmuring something to someone in the other room, or the delicious smell, but fortunately she didn't have to choose and followed both.

There was a room service table set up and Max was standing over by the large picture window, talking on the cell phone they'd purchased. From the sounds of it, he was talking to Drew Miller. She moved over to the table, sure he would fill her in when he got off the phone. She felt another little stab of guilt, knowing she couldn't be as sure she'd do the same, but suppressed it as she pulled a chair up to the table and sat down.

"Eat," Max mouthed, motioning with his hand for her to eat.

She did have pretty good manners and under normal circumstances, she would have been patient, but the smell of the food made her stomach growl. She selected a piece of bacon and crunched it, sighing at the immediate pleasure it brought to her tongue. Max ended his call and joined her at the table.

"Is he coming?" she asked, putting the bacon down as her stomach tightened a bit.

"In eight hours. He's got to catch a commercial flight

then get what he needs to get us off this island safe and sound. You going to be around in eight hours?"

"I deserved that."

"You want to tell me now what is going on?"

"Can we do it after breakfast? I don't want to ruin your appetite."

He grabbed her arm. "Now, Rio. It's long past due."

"I'd rather not ruin my appetite."

Max sighed.

She immediately rounded the breakfast cart, needing at least that much space separating them so she didn't feel so overwhelmed by his presence. "Okay." She looked him straight in the eye. "It's not the Ghost's men who are after us."

Unfortunately, the barrier didn't do much good. The man had an uncanny way of invading her personal space even when he was standing a good six feet away…with his beautiful blue eyes that seemed to touch her body like a caress and his warm male scent that filled every breath she inhaled.

She held his gaze, waiting for his anger to erupt and preparing herself for criticism and accusations. But all he did was stare at her, resentment and animosity mingling in his eyes—and something else she couldn't fully define. Hurt? Disappointment? Longing?

Oh, yes, there was definitely a hint of longing in his expression, and it was the brief glimpse of such a tangible emotion that was nearly her undoing. Despite her necessary actions, despite his own outrage over feeling deceived, he still wanted her.

Even if he didn't *want* to want her.

She thought her heart was going to break into a million pieces.

"But I thought that's why the DEA wanted me to be your bodyguard." His voice was low and rough.

"It wasn't, Max. I didn't really need a bodyguard."

She let that sink in. Tears pricked at the corners of her eyes, but she resolutely shoved them away. She was going to lose him over this. She knew that a long time ago, but now that it was happening, it was too much to bear.

His mouth tightened. "But that would mean there was another reason they wanted you out of L.A. Was it another mission?"

"Yes, I was given another mission."

"What is it? What were you supposed to do?"

"Distract you."

She watched as the knowledge seeped slowly into his eyes. He put his hands on the serving cart and leaned forward. "Me? Why the hell… The Ghost. This has something to do with the Ghost." He stiffened and abruptly straightened. He closed his eyes. "You baited me. Your whole story was fabricated. And I fell for it."

His eyes said, *I fell for you.*

"No, not the whole story. Everything I said really happened and it's possible I saw the Ghost. But he wasn't ever chasing me. I didn't think Eduardo would come after me and neither did the DEA."

When Max opened his eyes, Rio really wanted to run. Mixed in with the hurt and betrayal was anger she'd never seen before.

_10_

THE KNOWLEDGE HIT HIM like a sledgehammer. "You were bait," he repeated. Cursing himself for a fool. "What is this really about, Rio? And tell me the truth."

"You were looking to find and apprehend the Ghost. You wouldn't stop and you wouldn't listen. It put the DEA's whole operation in jeopardy. We have an agent deep undercover."

"So this is what you do for the agency…"

"No! It's not like that." She rounded the table and stood in front of him, her chin jutting out mutinously. "What happened with you and me in the forest was what I wanted. Not because of any mission I was given by the DEA. I got involved and I shouldn't have. I don't go around sleeping with men to do my job."

He glanced away and inhaled a deep breath, and when he looked at her again that harsh edge he was feeling inside hardened. He couldn't believe he had been so duped by her. The first time in his life when he'd trusted so completely. It served as a lesson. "All those words about trust I spouted to you? They meant nothing."

"You didn't really trust me, Max."

"How can you say that?"

"If you had, you'd have never pretended to go to sleep, and then followed me. I think you want to believe it's about trust, but it's about control for you. You should have just let me go."

"I couldn't let you go," he said, his voice a hard rasp. Grabbing hold of his anger was better than facing the truth. She'd lied to him, kept up the farce even after they'd gotten so close. But not close enough. Better to be angry than afraid. Better to push her away than to cling to her when he knew he'd lose her in the end anyway.

"You were loyal to the agency. I can't blame you for that. But I don't understand why you didn't trust me. After what happened between us? Don't you think you could have confided in me?"

She released a slow breath and said, "I know what's involved, Max. I understand your motivation. It doesn't change anything, but I understand it. This is about Allie. He almost got her killed."

His features tightened and he snapped, "And now Callie is going to assume her undercover identity, Gina Callahan, and will go after him once she's well enough. I didn't want my sister to face the monster."

The edge to his voice made her talk fast. "I know that must be eating you up inside."

"So the men who are after you…"

"Work for Eduardo Fuentes. We played up the Ghost stuff for your benefit, Max."

"Yeah," he said bitterly. "And I played right into it."

"Max—"

"No. I don't want your sympathy, Rio. I need some time to think."

He stalked away from her and left the room.

Outside in the hall, he headed blindly for the stairs instead of the elevator, needing the physical exercise to burn off the heat of his anger. She'd breached his trust and he had to live with that. He also had to live with the fact that he still wanted her. There were so many obstacles between the two of them, so many issues still left unresolved.... And did he even want to pursue her after finding out she'd been stringing him along since the very first second they met? Did she have a chance with him after lying to him on so many levels?

There were no easy answers for those nagging questions, just a voice in his head that told him Rio was worth his time and effort. Whatever was between them had the potential for developing into something stronger and bigger than the both of them. But he had to admit she was right about one thing. If he'd truly trusted her, he'd have really fallen asleep and then trusted her to take care of herself.

He had to grudgingly give her credit for the way she'd handled him. He had been on a single-minded mission to stop the Ghost before Callie had to get involved in the assignment to apprehend him. He wasn't sure anything— short of pulling him out of L.A. and giving him something else to occupy his mind—would have stopped him.

It didn't mean he was ready to forgive Rio for her part in it. When he hit the lobby, he started to jog. Slipping out the doors he headed for the beach.

RIO STARED AT THE DOOR, thinking that if she stared long enough, Max would come back and tell her he forgave her. Fat chance of that and she really should be more relieved than she was. Max wouldn't press her for anything now. As soon as they hit L.A., he'd want nothing more to do with her.

Damn—why did that hurt so much?

You've known him for how long? Three days?

Wow, was it only that? It seemed so much longer. The minutes and hours of the past two days had somehow been elongated, magnified and packed densely with need and fear. It seemed like forever, and at the same time, it could never be enough.

Fatigue pulled at her and she realized that getting some sleep was a better idea than standing here and second-guessing herself. What was done, was done.

She walked over to the bed and lay down, closing her eyes.

The dream hit her again. It wasn't so much a dream as a memory. They were at the beach, her parents and Shane. He was playing in the sand with her, packing buckets full and turning them over to form the castle.

As she played, the sky darkened and it was as if Shane shrank away from her. When she looked around, her parents had disappeared. Suddenly the storm hit, wind tore at her hair, rain lashed her skin with icy, hard pinpricks.

She called for Shane, but all she could see was a man in the shadows, that jaw, the bone structure, the powerful body.

Rio woke with a start and a headache. Her breath came in pants as the residual uneasiness of a dream hung around her. Eyes... She'd felt eyes on her, staring from the dark. But she hadn't been able to see his face, had only known somehow it was familiar.

It was only a dream, but the apprehension lingered as she sat up slowly and took stock of herself and the room around her. It had rained. The surface of the sliding glass door was spattered with windblown droplets. The weather system had moved on, but gray still clung to the sky.

She rubbed a hand over her face, groaning a bit as she had a headache. She didn't know how long she'd slept.

The sheets were torn loose from the foot of the bed, the spread rumpled.

Grimacing at the taste of bitter dreams in her mouth, she picked up the phone and ordered more food and some pills to take care of her headache.

Walking over to the now-cold breakfast, she poured herself a glass of juice. But before she could bring it to her mouth, it hit her like a speeding truck.

That face. The face she'd only glimpsed at Fuentes's—could it have been Shane?

"No, that was impossible." They'd buried him with honors as a hero. She'd seen the casket, seen him lowered into the ground. She'd put flowers on his grave for three years. She'd cried buckets of tears, vowed to bring his killer to justice. It wasn't possible.

But that man's bone structure had been so much like her brother's. She clutched her stomach as it twisted with the uneasiness of not being sure.

The juice glass fell from her suddenly nerveless fingers and pain crashed into her, her throat knotting from the shock.

Could he have been *working* for Fuentes? What could be the explanation? Was it possible her brother had betrayed them all and sided with a criminal?

He could very well be a traitor to his country, to her, to the memory of how they'd been raised.

It was too much to bear. With the emotional confession to Max about why they were really here in Maui and all the events of the last two days, Rio crumpled to the carpet, tears filling her eyes. Her world cracked, breaking foundations and tumbling her ideals.

Time slipped away as she sat there wondering, remembering, hurting, grieving. She let go of all the tears she had tried to hold on to, of all the pain she had been so afraid to feel. It came pouring out in a torrent, in a storm that shook her and drained her.

Right now she had no proof, no answers, but she intended to get them. As soon as she got back to L.A., she would confront the one man who had them. The director of the DEA, her boss.

Reeling with the information her brother could be working with Fuentes, Rio now understood: Shane was the Ghost. She really had seen the Ghost's face, and not only that, but the DEA also knew she posed a danger to them—that's why they made her distract Max. She could blow the whole undercover operation.

Wait a minute. Shane could be the undercover agent her boss had mentioned. She grabbed on to that thought like a lifeline. Would Shane do such a thing? Would he let her think he was dead for revenge of his own?

It was inconceivable her brother could now be on the wrong side of the law.

She needed answers. Was her brother dead or very much alive? Was he working for Fuentes or the DEA? Had everything she'd based her career on been a lie?

And she would get justice. She had to. If there was no justice, then all the suffering was for nothing. Senseless. Meaningless. There had to be justice. Even now, even too late, she wanted justice for herself and her parents.

She couldn't put the past behind her. It would never be forgotten, she vowed as old fears and new guilt settled inside her and solidified into a new strength.

There was a knock at the door and Rio stiffened and rose quickly to the backpack. Pulling out the Glock, she concealed it behind her and went to answer the door.

The bellman with the cart for the food stood on the other side of the door. She let him in, keeping the gun out of his sight and stashing it in the backpack as a pretense to getting the tip. He silently took the other food cart and handed her the bill. She signed it, tipped him and he left the room.

There was another knock and, taking no chances, she went through the whole routine again. Instead, Max was on the other side of the door. He looked damp and gorgeous, but his lean jaw was clenched tight. His dark hair was a disheveled, enticing mess around his head, as if he'd repeatedly combed through the strands with his fingers and left them to fall where they may. He looked so sinfully sexy he literally took her breath away.

"I forgot the key card."

Resolutely, she stepped aside and let him in.

He peered at her. "Are you okay?"

"I had a bad dream and I have a headache, but I'm fine," she lied. She had no intention of telling Max about Shane and that he could be working with Fuentes until she figured out her own feelings. Most important, she had no proof. And would he even trust her?

That thought just added to the pain she was already shouldering.

"Are you okay?" she asked pensively.

"You mean, have I gotten over my anger?"

"Yes."

"Somewhat."

She walked past Max, toward the enticing smell of food, hoping he would follow.

It surprised her, the strength of her desire to run to him, to smile into his face and hope he pulled her into his arms for a kiss. Like a normal couple. She didn't know what they were, but she doubted they were that. Too many complications. So she wasn't sure how to act.

He fell in beside her and her entire body responded to his nearness. Near the bed he pulled off the damp T-shirt and, using the towel from his shower, dried off.

"I guess you got caught in the rain."

"Yes. It was refreshing and cleared my head."

With deceptive laziness, he folded his arms across his broad, bare chest and leaned casually against the door frame, his entire demeanor cautious, and his guard in place. Not that she blamed him for being standoffish with her.

His indifference was exactly what she deserved, no matter how much she hated being on the receiving end of his aloof attitude. Even when she needed his warmth, his caring, his uncanny ability to make her feel so calm amidst the many burdens that weighed heavily on her conscience.

She picked up the hamburger and took a bite, chewing and moaning a little at the delicious tastes in her mouth.

"Looks good," he said, his husky tone giving away the fact he wasn't as unaffected by her presence as he'd like her to believe.

"Want a bite?" she offered.

A muscle in his cheek twitched, and a spark of anger flashed in his eyes that he'd welcome her so openly, so eagerly, when she'd kept so much from him.

"Please, take a bite," she pleaded, knowing it wasn't about the hamburger at all. It felt so much like Eve offering the apple to Adam, but in this case it didn't have anything to do with the devil and everything to do with them.

She splayed her free hand against his hard, virile chest, her impulsive reaction effectively cutting off whatever he'd been about to say. Rio had the sinking feeling his next words would have been too devastating to hear.

He must have heard the raw emotion in her voice because something in his expression softened, and he reached out for the burger in her other hand and took a bite.

Without another word, she slid her flattened hand up his taut chest, along his shoulder, and curled her fingers along his nape. Silently, she pulled his mouth down to her parted lips and kissed him—soft, lush kisses that grew hotter, wetter, more daring—until with an unrefined groan of surrender he responded.

She might have been the initiator, but it wasn't long

before Max took control, and she gladly let him. He backed her up against the nearest wall. Removing the burger and setting it down on the table, he pressed his hard, fully aroused body against hers as his mouth claimed and devoured with ravenous greed. He molded her hips in his hands, his fingers biting into her flesh through the cotton of her shorts as he shifted her closer, then slid the muscular length of his thigh between her legs, forcing them apart, forcing her to endure the strong, steady rhythm and friction against her sex.

She felt the rush of moisture, and the heat between them flared with startling suddenness—like a flame touched to dry kindling. An orgasm built, but just as her climax increased in aching need, Max pulled his mouth from hers and removed his leg, leaving her on the verge of an exquisite release.

Breathing hard, his eyes blazing hot, he held her heavy-lidded gaze with his own and began unfastening the buttons on her shirt. His fingers stroked her skin, the swell of her breast, the deep valley in between, as he slowly made his way downward to her stomach.

He dragged the sides of her shirt down her arms, along with the straps of her pink bra, until both caught in the crook of her arms. Then he pushed the lacy cups down, freeing her full, aching breasts to his gaze. Her nipples tightened painfully, and she arched her back until the tender peaks scraped across his naked chest.

The sensation jolted her, teased her, but that brush of contact wasn't enough. "Max," she moaned, flushed and panting with the excruciating need to experience more.

"Don't fret, Rio." Dropping his head, he lightly bit

her full lower lip, and then soothed the sting with a damp, silky stroke of his tongue before moving his mouth up to her ear.

"I'm going to take you," he said, his voice rough and wholly male. "With my fingers, then my mouth, and finally, my cock."

"Max," she gasped. "Yes."

"There's much more between us than this," he said softly. "When it comes to you, Rio. I have no defenses."

Her eyes stung, knowing that she craved him as much as he craved her, but she didn't know where it could lead.

He thrust and gyrated his hips against hers, driving home to her that he had what it took to back up his erotic threat.

He framed her jaw in his big hands, holding her steady as he tipped her face up to his. The bright flare of hunger in his stare and the dark, edgy beauty of his aroused expression stole her breath and incited another surge of liquid heat between her thighs, priming her for what lay ahead.

"I know you're sorry about lying to me."

"I am, Max. I truly am."

The last thing she saw was the satisfaction in his gaze before he captured her lips with his, and this time the kiss was hard, fierce and deeply carnal right from the initial onslaught. She felt his primitive need to be in control, to dominate, to possess her completely. It was exactly what she craved, and she gave herself to him freely, without inhibitions, holding nothing back.

He continued to plunder her mouth with the hot,

voracious sweep of his tongue, making her melt, inside and out. His hands dropped to the button on her shorts and he impatiently released it and the zipper to shove her shorts off.

Then he ripped her brand-new underwear as if it were tissue paper. She gasped in shock, and he swallowed the sound as his palm skimmed up her quivering thigh with driving purpose. Two long, thick fingers slid inside her, filling her up, and his thumb strummed across her pulsing clit.

Wrenching his mouth from hers with a low growl, he bent his head to her breast and latched on to a nipple, biting her softly. He suckled her, hard and strong, creating a tugging, rippling sensation that spiraled down to where his fingers were stroking and gliding within her. Then his thumb joined in the foray, so knowing and skillful, and so intent on pushing her to dizzying heights of pleasure.

Feeling as though she needed to hang on to something solid, she pushed her hands through his hair and twisted her fingers into the soft curls just as need coiled through her body with a ferocity she didn't recognize. She tipped her head back against the wall, and cried out as her orgasm crested and a blissful warmth shimmied through her in waves.

Just when she was certain she was going to collapse to the floor, Max smoothed his hands over her bare bottom and grasped the backs of her thighs, bending her knees as he lifted her off the ground.

"Wrap your legs around my waist," he told her, his voice strained with his own barely contained passion.

She managed that much at least and was amazed at

his strength and stamina as he took her in his arms and carried her down to the bed.

But he wasn't done with her yet, she knew, as he tumbled her unceremoniously onto the bed, then grabbed her ankles and dragged her to the edge of the mattress so her legs dangled over the side. Absently, she reached up and skimmed her fingers over her engorged nipples, which were still damp from his mouth and tongue. She teased him, teased herself, and he stared at her naked body with hungry eyes, seducing her mind and senses right along with the rest of her.

Not so surprisingly, another spiral of desire curled within her as his promise of the various ways he planned to take her echoed in her mind, along with her acquiescence so far. She prepared herself for the second round of pleasure, certain he'd be just as ruthless in his attempt to make her come as he'd been moments ago.

He dropped to his knees in front of her and pushed her thighs wide open with his splayed palms, then used his thumb to spread open her sex, exposing her completely. He leaned forward, and she closed her eyes, feeling a gust of hot breath, then the velvet-soft glide of his tongue along her wet, swollen cleft. He closed his mouth over her, kissing her intimately, deeply, using his tongue in ways that were wonderfully wicked and shockingly erotic. He manipulated her clit with those clever thumbs of his again, pressing, rubbing, stroking. It was almost more than she could stand.

Those familiar tremors undulated through her, his seductive effect on her inescapable. Moaning softly, she gave herself over to his unrelenting mouth and his swirling, thrusting tongue.

Even before the sweet aftershocks of her orgasm had time to subside, he was standing between her legs, towering over her, his fingers ripping open the front placket of his shorts. She watched in dreamy awe as the finely honed muscles across his well-defined chest and along his arms bunched and flexed with his quick movements.

Once the buttons were undone, he shoved the material and his boxers to his thighs. He had his thick cock in his hand, clearly planning to take her to greater heights on the wing of her previous vow.

He hooked his arms beneath the crooks of her knees so she was wide open to him and he was in complete control. The broad head of his shaft glided through her slippery wetness, unerringly found the entrance to her body and pressed in an excruciating inch.

His face was drawn with such raw, sexual need, and she clutched at the covers at her sides as an anchor, expecting the pleasure of his first thrust to be overwhelming.

But nothing could prepare her for the way his body covered her, the way he braced his forearms on either side of her shoulders, which kept her splayed legs trapped against the muscled weight of his body, the unyielding strength of his chest. It also made for a tighter fit, she realized, as he speared forward and impaled himself to the hilt, stealing her breath at the same time.

He dropped his head against her neck and groaned as he forced his way deeper, if that was even possible. She shuddered at the sensation of being filled so completely and closed her eyes, her back bowing as he began to move in earnest, his strokes growing faster, harder, stronger…

"Look into my eyes," he demanded in a hoarse whisper.

Dazed, she opened her eyes. His face was inches away from hers as he continued to thrust into her, his blue eyes so intense they burned straight to her soul, and she knew in that moment she'd never be the same again.

He reached up and tangled his fingers in her hair, his lips next to her, ear and whispered words that were rough, demanding and oh-so-explicit.

Come for me.

She was already there, her orgasm slamming into her with the same amount of force he was. She cried his name over and over as her entire body convulsed around him, beneath him, giving him the same pleasure he was sure to see in her eyes. He was in tune with her, stiffening at the height of her climax, his head thrown back and a low, guttural groan ripping from his throat.

Long minutes later, he released her legs from their awkward position, but didn't move off her, and amazingly, she could still feel him pulsing inside her. He stared down at her, his features harsh despite the recent release that should have eased the tension thrumming through him.

"I'll get you back to L.A. After that you call the shots. I'll abide by whatever decision you make."

She'd craved the closeness, the physical intimacy, the emotional connection that only he seemed able to give her. And it had all been there in varying degrees, stunning in its intensity.

"Are you sure you can do that?"

He closed his eyes. "For you, Rio, I can try. I've done some thinking and you were right. It is about control. I don't trust anyone to do the job I can do. I don't put faith in other people."

"Will you let me explain?"

He settled them in a more comfortable position, wrapping his arms around her.

"If it will make you feel better."

"It will."

"Shoot."

"My brother, Shane, died during a mission with the DEA. Fuentes killed him. The reason I accepted this job to distract you is because the DEA has an agent under-cover right now working to topple Fuentes. I had to help. I couldn't bear it if I was the cause of another agent dying at Fuentes's hands. Do you understand?"

"Yes, I understand."

She could tell by his voice he might understand, but he hadn't quite come to terms with her duplicity. She couldn't blame him. Suddenly everything seemed so overwhelming. Tears gathered in her eyes and she let them fall.

"Sweetheart, don't cry."

"I discovered something while you were gone."

"What?"

"I think Shane is working for Fuentes. I'm almost convinced he's the man I saw at the compound. That's why he looked so familiar."

"Your brother is the Ghost?"

"I don't know," she cried softly. "I only saw him in the dark, in shadow. I haven't seen him in three years and I thought he was dead. But I must have known on some level. That's why I had those dreams—always of Shane receding into shadow, disappearing…like a ghost."

"But you're still not sure?"

"No, Max. I'm not sure and it's killing me. I intend to get some answers from my boss when I get back to L.A. I know it's going to be difficult with the mole and all."

"I think I know someone who can help us with the mole problem."

"Who?"

"An exterminator."

Max grabbed the cell and had a brief conversation with Drew, who promised to put his best man on the job.

"That's helpful, Max," Rio said. "But, if I have to, I'll go over my boss's head and cause a stink until I get some answers."

"That might not be a good idea."

"I think he set us both up. I would distract you and you'd be just as much of a distraction to me. He wanted us both out of the way."

"You could lose your job."

"I don't care. If the DEA won't give me the answers I want, then I'll go to Colombia. I'll track down this Ghost and then I'll be sure."

"If what you believe is true, then it makes me want to hunt the Ghost even more. To give us both closure."

"I can get my own closure, Max," she said before she thought better of it.

"Right. Forgot, you're the one who doesn't need anyone's help."

11

I CAN GET MY OWN CLOSURE.

Max couldn't shake those words. It was clear to him Rio had issues, emotional baggage, whatever it was called.

During their conversation about her brother, her barriers had fallen, revealing something surprisingly vulnerable beneath that confident surface. Then she'd popped those barriers back in place, reinforced with anger.

He played it back, examining his own feelings a little deeper. Her lying still hurt but the betrayal he'd felt was assuaged by her reasons for deceiving him.

It was totally understandable to want to protect a fellow agent and doubly so when he'd found out Rio had lost her DEA brother to Fuentes.

Or had she?

Was her brother a traitor? Was he really dead and her imagination was taking her places? Could he be the Ghost?

Max didn't know for certain, but what chilled him was Rio would attempt to get answers no matter what.

What he did know was that he was in love with her, but he wasn't sure he could trust her a second time. She was hell-bent on her own personal mission. And dammit he understood that, too. He wanted the Ghost out of the picture so Callie wouldn't have to put herself in danger.

He stared out the windshield as he maneuvered the car around the dangerous curves in the road, thinking about the dangerous curves in his own life.

As concerned and confused as he was, he found himself smiling. So she was angry at him for trying to help her. It wasn't necessarily a bad thing, because that kind of anger could be fueled only by one thing: passion. If he didn't matter, he wouldn't rate that kind of response.

All he had to do now was get her to the airport and on that waiting chopper. Drew was a genius and he'd already taken care of all the arrangements. He would fly them off Maui to Honolulu where they were booked on a commercial flight to LAX. From there, Max had every intention of going with Rio straight to the DEA and her boss.

He had to hold fast to the knowledge that while she was busy saying no and constructing a wall, in that moment when she'd looked into his eyes, there had been confusion and longing plainly there for him to see. And that said otherwise. That had given him hope. Whatever was going on deep inside that beautiful brain of hers, she didn't want to admit he mattered.

He could wait. He was patient.

"Is your almost brother-in-law good enough to get us off the island?"

Max settled back in the driver's seat. "He got you out of Colombia in one piece, didn't he?"

"I guess he did. I don't remember a thing."

"Miller was a freelance black ops mercenary when he met my sister Allie. He's a former army Ranger...."

She gave him a sidelong, amused glance. "Former? So only marines are marines for life?"

Max chuckled. "That's right—*Semper fidelis,* baby."

"This guy sounds like an American James Bond," she said, rolling down the window. The scent of sweet flowers and sunshine filled the air inside the car.

"He's damn good and from what I've gathered can fly anything from a glider to a jumbo 747," Max said grudgingly.

"Oh, ho, sounds like his invitation to the family might have gotten lost in the mail?"

Max couldn't help but smile, but he kept his eyes on the road. "At first I wasn't too crazy about having a black ops guy around, but he gave that up for my sister."

"What's he doing now?" Rio shifted around in her seat to better face him.

"Training recruits for a top secret agency."

"Watchdog?"

Max snorted. "You know?"

Rio nodded. "I read the file and I know who got me out of Columbia."

He glanced at her and was struck by her beauty. He had to restrain himself from reaching out and touching her. "The DEA did a good job of debriefing you."

They rode in silence for a few more minutes and it was comfortable between them. He got her to open up a little about her childhood. She glowed when she spoke of her parents, especially her father, and seemed to relax a little. Max wasn't typically one to talk about himself, much less his childhood, and when he did, he was usually gauging every word. With her, however, it felt natural. Effortless. Incredibly so, in fact.

He slowed the car down as he navigated the road that led to the airport, where there was a helpful sign embossed with a plane. And he watched as the tension tightened her up again.

The more time he spent with her, the more he wanted of her. Preferably without the haunted look in her eyes. He supposed in order to get what he wanted, he was going to have to slay some dragons. Whether she wanted him to or not.

Now that they were close to getting off the island, he broached the subject that hadn't been far from his mind. "Have you thought about what Fuentes wants from you?"

"No, I can't imagine what it is that's got him so worked up. He was so livid when we met."

Max's brows rose. She was a closemouthed little thing. "You met?"

She gave an impatient sigh and he noted her hands tightened in her lap. "Yes, he was the one I was fighting when you got shot."

Max smiled a purely smug smile. "You kicked his ass?"

She matched his smile, her eyes lighting up. "Yes, I did. I was contemplating putting a bullet in his brain when you came along and distracted me."

Max's smile faded and he gave her a quick glance. "Remind me never to get on your bad side."

She shrugged. "I couldn't do it. Not really. I'd rather

see him tried for all the pain and suffering he's caused so many people and their families."

"Why do you think he was so pissed?"

She was quiet for so long he didn't think she was going to answer. "I think his pride has been hurt that a lowly woman escaped his compound. I have to admit it doesn't look good that I escaped. Drug lords cannot afford to look weak in any way."

"Do you think there might be a connection to Fuentes that you're not aware of?" It was a fishing expedition because he believed there was something there. He didn't want to make her angry. Ultimately, he was more concerned about figuring out what was going on. Knowledge was power.

"Like?"

"The real mission you were on before those monkeyshines got you into a whole lot of trouble." He pulled into a parking space in front of the airport and turned off the engine.

She swatted at his arm. "You think your monkey jokes are funny, huh?"

"Yeah," he said with a quick grin. "Give. The real mission?"

She glanced over at him, clearly uncomfortable. "Max, it goes against my oath."

"I would agree with you, but I'm a federal agent, Rio. I also took an oath. It would be good to understand all the pieces here."

She held his gaze for a fraction of a second, and then dipped her chin in quick, silent agreement. "I was working undercover with a member of the Defensores de la Libertad. There was a rumor that Fuentes was teaming up with them as his new security force. I was supposed to infiltrate them, with the help of my informant, and find out what I could about the agreement. It was purely an information-gathering mission."

"But our little howler threw a monkey wrench into your plans."

"Max!"

He looked at her, and then noticed the tiniest of twitches at the corner of her mouth. "Couldn't resist. So what did you tell him when he questioned you?"

She grinned at him. "I told him I was sightseeing. He didn't think it was funny."

"I bet you'd spit in the devil's eye and tell him to go to hell."

She laughed. "Max, he's already in hell."

"My point exactly."

She folded her arms across her chest, all humor gone. Looking out at the movement of traffic and people running to catch flights, she worried her bottom lip. "Getting back to Fuentes—it wasn't even until later that he discovered I was a DEA agent. I suspect that was due to the mole."

"So, maybe it is this Libertad thing that's gotten him so gung ho to capture you alive?"

She thought for a moment and then looked at him. "It could be. I hope I don't find out the hard way."

"You won't if you stick to the plan."

"I'll stick, Max. I want answers from my boss. Girl Scout promise."

"Well, if you're going to invoke the Girl Scout promise…I'm convinced," he said wryly.

He picked up the throwaway cell phone he'd bought in Wailea and pressed the numbers Drew had given him.

Drew answered on the first ring. "Max?"

"Yes, we're here parked in the spot you said. What now?"

"I'm sending two of my people. Jason Kyoto will take care of the rental. You get into the vehicle with a big Aussie named Thad Michaels. He'll bring you to the hangar."

Max heard the frustration in Drew's voice. "What's up?"

"Nothing I can't handle. Just get your asses here pronto. I've seen enough dangerous guys around here to be nervous."

Even as he spoke, a car stamped with Airport Security pulled up. An Asian man exited the car and came up to the driver's-side window.

Max rolled it down. "Kyoto?"

He nodded. "Leave the key in the ignition. Let's move."

Max nodded at Rio and they got out of the car and walked over to the other vehicle. Once inside, they nodded to the driver. "Michaels?"

Thad nodded and shook Max's hand.

"Thanks for coming."

"I follow the captain's orders, mate, but glad to help. Buckle in. I'd suggest the pretty sheila duck down in the seat. They'll be looking closely at any man-and-woman combo, especially one with such lovely red hair."

Rio slid down into the seat until she was effectively out of sight.

"There's a holdup, I'm afraid," Thad said as he maneuvered the car through the security gates into the back of the airport and toward the heliport area.

"Nothing ever goes as smoothly as planned."

"True blue, mate, but no worries. Drew will fix it."

THAD DROVE UP TO ONE of the hangars and waited while they got out. "I'll be back," he said, flashing a brilliant smile. "I've got to get Jason. Drew's inside."

They entered the hangar and were assaulted by the smell of grease and fuel. A man in a blue jumpsuit was working on a helicopter hooked up to a tug.

The man swore and turned. Catching Max's eye, he dropped the wrench into the toolbox and picked up a rag to wipe off his hands. He walked over and shook Max's hand.

"Sorry, complication. I never fly a bird until I check it over and this one needed a repair before I flew over hundreds of miles of ocean. It won't take more than another twenty minutes." A woman, armed to the teeth, came around the tail of the chopper.

"All clear, Captain," she said.

"Leila Mendez," Drew said, and then he looked past Max's shoulder directly at Rio.

"We haven't been properly introduced. Drew Miller."

Lethal in both looks and expertise, Rio thought. "It's a pleasure to finally meet you and now I can thank you personally for saving my life—twice."

"Sure, no problem." Drew turned back to Max. "There's an office back there we can use and, unfortunately, only a vending machine if you're hungry. As soon as Thad and Jason get back, they'll join Leila. I'd better get at that chopper."

When he drew abreast of Max again, he said under his breath, "Keep her out of sight."

Rio couldn't help but bristle at that. She wasn't a damsel in distress here. She was a government agent and she didn't like being talked about in the third person.

"I know enough to stay out of sight and I'd appreciate it if any plans that are made include me."

Drew looked at her with a little more respect in his eyes. "Yes, ma'am," he said, gave Max a smile and went back to the helicopter.

Leila Mendez said, "She put you in your place, Drew."

"Shut up, Leila, and check the perimeter again."

"Yes, sir," she said as she headed for the hangar doors, throwing Rio a quick smile.

"You really are something," Max said as he took her arm and started to lead her to the office.

"I also can walk by myself, Max. I've been doing it since I was one. I've got the hang of it now."

She wasn't sure why she was in such a snit. But, true to form, Max wasn't going to let her off easily.

"What was that all about?"

"What?" Rio asked as she opened the office door and went inside. He got in front of her and she sidestepped him, but he grabbed her elbow and spun her to face him.

"You know Drew's here to help you. As a favor to me. There's no need to act like that."

"I don't want to be treated like I'm not part of this. I'm the main part, Max."

She tugged her elbow free, fervently hoping he took

the diversionary tactic at face value, even while silently apologizing to him. She knew he did want to help her. But she hated it, hated that all these people were involved and in danger because of her.

She turned away, but he took her straight into his arms, pulling her flush up against him.

"Let me go," she demanded.

"I will. As soon as you let me talk."

"Fine." She tried not to look him directly in the eye, to focus on some point just to the side of his face, but he wouldn't allow that. Maybe he did understand her, because while he was clearly not happy with her just then, he was also not conceeding an inch and she had to give him grudging respect for that.

"You don't want all these people here to rescue you, do you?" And just like that, he gentled his voice, gentled his touch. "I'm trained for the subtle signals, too, you know. You're upset." He lifted a hand to her face, and despite every instinct she had screaming at her to move away, she let him touch her.

It was no brief, tingling caress—his touch was warm and steadying…as well as stimulating and electrifying. It was more than she could handle. "Yes, dammit, Max. The responsibility of all these lives." Her voice was wobbling, but he'd have had that effect on her even if she wasn't hanging by a thread.

Instead, he leaned in and kissed her, gently but thoroughly, lifting his head again before she could decide what to do about it.

"I'm not sure I can get used to this, Max," she said, her voice reedy, her body shaking.

"Yes, you can. It's all about practice. I can make you believe that it's better together."

"Not in my experience," she murmured, desperately wanting to have the strength to resist this, to resist him.

"We'll have to talk about that."

And that was just it. Looking at him, so steady, so strong-willed, so profoundly sure of himself. So very sure of her. The very depth of need she'd developed for him, so swiftly, was more terrifying than the predicament she was already involved in. That alone was reason enough to step back. "I appreciate the offer, I do," she said quietly. "But like I said I don't think I could get used to it."

She slowly extricated herself from his arms. This time he let her go. And, perversely, her heart constricted.

He didn't look remotely convinced and somewhere in her stupid heart she rejoiced.

She said nothing more. She'd already said far too much.

"Want something from the vending machine?"

"Candy bar with peanuts."

She watched him turn and stroll out of the office. Just before passing through the door, he turned. "Think about what I said, Rio. About everything I said."

Rio sat down on the couch. When she wasn't worrying about the situation with Fuentes and thinking about how she was going to get the bastard, she was thinking about Max and how much she wanted to let go and love him. Really love him with no strings attached and no baggage.

But she had baggage. She had plenty of it. She

couldn't go through it again, losing someone she loved. Making a life with Max beckoned like a beautiful jewel, but her fear held her paralyzed.

She wasn't sure what to think anymore…. Was Shane alive, and if so, was he a traitor or a hero? Again she wondered if perhaps he was the undercover agent that needed protection. That would be the best scenario.

Rio got up and peered through the glass of the office. Max had gotten her candy, but he was talking to Drew, who was closing up the panel of the helicopter.

Thank God. It was time to go. She reached for the door handle at the same time a blast ripped through the warehouse. The glass in the office exploded and the report from the detonation threw Rio away from the door. She landed on her back, her senses reeling and her ears throbbing.

She heard footsteps and crunching glass just before someone grabbed her hair and yanked her against him, her back to his chest. Her scalp on fire, an instant later she felt the cold muzzle of his gun against her temple. His voice next to her ear made her shudder.

"*Hola,* Agent Marshall. We meet again."

Rio elbowed him in the ribs, but Fuentes only grunted and pushed the gun harder to her temple.

"Do not test me more than you already have." His fist was still in her hair, and tears sprang to the corners of her eyes as he gave it a vicious twist. "Now I will release you, and you will do as I say, when I say. Are we understood?" To underscore the questions, he tugged her even more tightly against him.

"Yes," she choked out. She was thinking only of

Max. She wanted to rush from the room and find him, assure herself he was alive.

"Good," Fuentes said quite pleasantly, and released her as suddenly as he'd grabbed her.

She staggered forward and landed hard on her hands and knees on the linoleum floor.

"Get up. Time is precious. We must go."

She scrambled up, wanting to keep her eyes on him at all times.

"Go where?"

"Back to Colombia where I can, once again, bestow on you my excellent hospitality. *Mi casa, su casa,* no?"

Her heart started to pound in her chest and fear edged up her throat, squeezing it tight.

"I'd rather not. I don't care for your accommodations—the food sucked."

He laughed, and then backhanded her across the face.

She felt her lip split, but when the pain subsided, she gave him no quarter with a hard glare.

"Ah, it seems you are one to be broken. Fear not, *gato,* I will use up your nine lives."

He grabbed her elbow and shoved her roughly ahead of him. "Walking, no talking. Not until we're clear of the warehouse."

Pain kicked hard at her heart when she couldn't see Max and his friends because of all the dust and debris. She could only hope they were all alive. Especially Max. She wanted to cry for the man, for the lover, for the scattered moments in this crazy Maui trip they might have made into more. If she'd thought she'd loved before, those illusions were all blasted away. It had been all too brief.

She hadn't realized she'd stopped walking. A vicious shove sent her sprawling. Fuentes and his goons laughed. She pushed to her feet, her eyes searching for Max. A scream bubbled in her throat, the agony of not knowing if she'd lost him raking at her heart.

"Walk."

She stumbled with another push. Once out of the hangar she was forced into a waiting vehicle and driven to a sleek private jet that sat on the runway.

She asked, "What do you want with me?"

"Answers to my questions, *gato*. If I don't get what I want from you the first time, I'll ask over and over again."

For a split second all those terrible memories of torture came flooding in and her mouth went dry.

He pushed her out of the car and ushered her up the stairs of the plane. Once inside, he buckled her in.

"Wouldn't want anything to happen to you, would we?" He laughed. Then he sat down next to her, keeping the gun trained on her the whole time.

She was dependent on Max to find her. If Max and the others were dead, there was likely to be no rescue at all. That meant her survival depended solely on her and for the first time that thought held no appeal at all.

MAX WOKE SLOWLY. His brain felt like someone had been playing tennis with it. His ears rang and his vision was a bit blurred. He sat up and felt dizzy, then held himself still until the sensation passed. Then he spotted Drew and his team sprawled on the hangar floor. He checked each person and breathed easier to find out they were all alive.

Oh God. Rio!

He rose, ignoring the pain in his head, and ran to the office. The door had been blown off its hinges, glass crunching under his feet.

Rio was gone. He broke apart inside for just an instant. He would have taken her alive.

"Max," Drew said weakly as he came up to him.

"She's gone. Fuentes has taken her." Max felt his heart pounding in his chest. After all the words he'd spouted about helping her, he'd failed her.

"What the hell happened?" asked Jason.

"Concussion grenades. They used them so Rio wouldn't be harmed in a gun battle," Max growled.

"Smart." Drew looked at Max. "So what do we do now, Carpenter?"

"We go after her and if he's harmed her, there's going to be one less drug lord in Colombia."

"Works for me," Drew said as they all headed toward the chopper.

12

SHE KNEW WHERE SHE WAS.

Cartagena, Colombia. She recognized the city she'd spent a lot of time in, with its bright bougainvillea tumbling from colonial balconies and the shimmering Caribbean looking like a jewel.

They took her from the plane and bound her hands and feet before gagging her and throwing her into the back of a covered pickup truck. The drive was completely unpleasant as she couldn't brace herself at turns, which aggravated the bumps, bruises and cuts that stung and ached all over her exhausted body.

But she understood this was just a precursor to what she would have to endure. Wherever they were taking her was going to be much, much worse.

She was terrified of what they were going to do to her, but she had handled it the first time around. She would handle it now.

She thought about Max and what they had shared from the moment they'd had to flee Fuentes's men. She thought about what she would have thrown away if Fuentes hadn't captured her. She would have walked away from Max because of her own fear of losing him.

Now she realized the time she spent with Max would have been worth anything. There were never any guarantees in life.

She acknowledged that recent events could end up robbing her of finding out just what they might have had together, but that didn't stop her from thinking about what she'd want, if it were up to her.

Max, if he was alive, would come after her. She knew it in her heart. A sob caught in her throat as she thought about losing him, and that maybe it was too late for them, but she fortified herself with the secure knowledge Max just wouldn't let her down.

The truck stopped moving and adrenaline surged into Rio's system. The back door opened and she was unceremoniously dragged from the bed of the truck onto the ground.

The impact jarred her ribs and she moaned behind the gag. When the pain subsided, she looked around. She was in back of a beautiful villa.

"Welcome to my home, whore. Rojo por la Mañana."

Red in the morning. The sunrise here must be quite beautiful to turn the stucco walls of the villa red. What a lovely name for a place where she'd find her end.

"Take her to a cell," Fuentes said in a clipped tone, and she was picked up by one of the guards and taken into the building.

Once inside, she was shown down a hallway to the back of the place where there were a row of cells. She tried to mentally prepare herself; she wasn't going to let this intimidate her. She refused to make a sound when he dropped her onto the hard packed dirt floor.

He removed her bonds and her gag and then left, locking the door behind him.

She was going to believe that it was only a matter of time before Max found her and saved her. She only had to hold out until then. She wasn't going to think about him being dead.

BACK IN L.A., MAX paced another hangar as Drew's team prepared to go to Colombia.

"Are you sure you don't want to consult the FBI, Max?" Drew asked for the tenth time. "I have an open ticket with Watchdog. Anything I need I get, but the FBI will crucify you if they find out that you're going into Colombia without authorization."

"The DEA isn't going to be crazy about it, either," Jason said, hauling a black duffel up the ramp of the jet.

"I was supposed to protect her," Max said, trying not to let his desperation show.

"Still, you could lose your…"

"No. I can't go to the FBI or DEA. Remember the mole in the operation somewhere? Whoever it is will tip off Fuentes we're coming. I can't risk the agency telling me to stay put and waste time while they decide what to do about Rio. We go."

"Max," Drew cautioned, "I'm with you on this all the way. I just thought you might want to consider your job."

"I don't give a damn about my job right now. All that matters is getting Rio out of there. You know as well as I do that once they get what they want out of her they're going to kill her. All we have right now is time. The faster we get to her, the better her chances are."

"Okay." Drew held up his hands in mock surrender.

A dark-haired man with a short ponytail entered the hangar dressed in black and carrying a laptop case. Drew waved him over. "This is Damian Frost. He's a genius with a computer. He'll find out where that jet landed and he's also the one who's been working on your mole."

Max nodded to Damian. "Thanks, man."

"No problem."

The Irish accent threw him for a minute, then he remembered Allie talking about all the operatives that had helped her through her mission with the Ghost. Jason Kyoto was Japanese and had been her former assistant until she'd found out that Callie had hired him to be her bodyguard. Leila Mendez, a martial arts expert, had escaped Colombia to become a top field agent. Thad Michaels had saved the president's life and was a former boxer and Australian Special Forces guy who'd turned mercenary, and Damian Frost was former IRA. Certainly an interesting group of people. They had all been recruited by Watchdog.

Minutes later they boarded the plane and Drew got behind the controls and took off.

Jason looked over at Max. "Are you familiar with body armor and assault weapons?"

"Yes. I'm a marine. You don't have to worry about me."

Jason smiled. "Freaking A. You guys know how to kick some serious ass."

DREW'S EXCELLENT OPERATIVE, Damian Frost, had traced the jet to Cartagena. Hours later, they had just checked in to a hotel room there when Drew's phone rang. Drew answered, "Yeah."

He looked at Max with a shocked look on his face. "It's for you."

"What?" Max took the phone and put it to his ear. "Who is this?"

"It doesn't matter who I am," a man said, his voice low and steely. "I have information you want regarding a very beautiful DEA agent."

"Rio. Where is she?" Max demanded, his heart rolling over in his chest.

"I'll tell you this information, but I have two conditions."

"Name them," Max growled.

"No one touches Eduardo Fuentes. If he dies, I'll make it very unpleasant for you."

"I hear you. And the other condition?"

"Stop pursuing the Ghost, Mr. Carpenter. It's a futile search and a waste of your time."

"Is *this* the Ghost?" Max asked, thinking how much danger Callie was going to face if he didn't get to the Ghost first. "Are you Rio's brother, Shane?"

There was a long pause and Max thought he might have blown it. Then the man spoke. "Shane McMasters no longer exists. I already told you. It doesn't matter who I am." Impatience laced his voice.

Max clutched the phone until his hand turned white. He wanted to throttle the man whose voice was so calm. He knew in his churning gut this was the Ghost. He wanted to make the man a ghost for real. He thought of

Rio, of the terror she was suffering at the hands of Fuentes. "Tell me where Rio is."

"I'll have your word first, Mr. Carpenter."

"What makes you think I'll keep my word once Rio is safe?" Max scoffed.

"You will. That's the kind of man you are. Do we have a deal?"

"We have a deal," Max said through gritted teeth.

"She's being held in the villa Rojo por la Mañana. It's about twenty miles west out of the city of Cartagena. Be quick, Mr. Carpenter. She is much too beautiful to die."

Max's heart bucked violently, fury causing it to beat harder. Savagely, he cursed and closed the phone with a snap.

"I know where she is," he announced. After a moment, Max turned to Damian Frost. "I really need you to find that mole, Mr. Frost."

"Aye, I've been flat out with the search," Frost said as he intertwined his fingers and cracked his knuckles, grinning at Max. "You go save your good lady and I'll get back to it." He started tapping on the keys of his laptop.

JAMMER CLOSED THE CHEAP throwaway phone he'd used to talk to Max Carpenter. Dropping it on the ground, he gave it a quick crack with his boot heel, laughing softly. Let Eduardo find it and worry whether it was one of his people using it to betray him.

"You have a traitor in your midst, Eduardo." That hadn't been a lie. Standing outside of the back of the villa, Jammer caught the guard who exited the cells. In perfect Spanish, he warned, "You touch her in any way that violates her and I'll kill you."

"What do you care for this woman?"

"She's more likely to talk if she's treated well. Do I make myself clear?"

"You are clear."

Jammer peered at the woman through the small window. He'd done all he could for her; he let the emotion he felt slip free of the tight reins. Shane was gone, but his sister was very much alive. He prayed that Max Carpenter loved her as much as Jammer thought he did, since her life now depended on him.

Jammer also hoped he'd pegged the FBI agent's character and he would leave Eduardo alive as promised. As the Ghost, he'd worked way too hard to put all this together to lose it now. He was close to selling Fuentes the biggest shipment of armaments he'd ever assembled. It would support Fuentes's bid to be one of the richest drug lords in Colombia. For Fuentes, securing a partnership with the Defensores de la Libertad would guarantee his operation's success and make him untouchable. That's exactly what the Ghost was hoping for. It would make destroying Fuentes so much sweeter. Just a bit longer and Jammer would have what he wanted.

He hoped that Max Carpenter got what he wanted, too.

RIO DIDN'T KNOW HOW long she'd been lying on the dirt floor. She'd been passing the time fantasizing about Max. She remembered his mouth, so soft and clever and the way he knew how to put it to good use. She remembered his warm, sure hands running over her, making her fidget and moan.

The sound of footsteps made her shoot up from the floor. A man appeared in front of her cell.

"It's about time," she croaked. "I called down for extra towels an hour ago."

The guard chuckled, pinning her with a knowing gaze, and Rio stood stolidly, ignoring all the painful places on her body.

He entered the cell and clamped bright silver handcuffs on her, then motioned her ahead. Rio moved past him, thinking what a waste this was because she wasn't giving up any information.

The guard gripped her arm and pushed her forward.

"What's with all the shoving?" she complained.

He just pushed her again.

"Vamos," he snapped, crowding behind her as she was ushered to a room with nothing in it but a chair and a table. She caught a glimpse of the gorgeous setting outside. The sight seemed so surreal compared to the crudeness of her cell.

"I will ask you questions. You will answer these questions or you will be punished," the soldier informed her.

"Are you going to put me in a time-out?"

"No," he said, and then backhanded her. "Does this clear it up?"

"That makes it very clear."

"Good. Now who is the traitor in Mr. Fuentes's compound? Who has been informing on him?"

"I don't know what you're talking about."

"I warn you, *señorita*. I do not play games."

"I'm not playing games. I don't have the information you seek."

He slapped her again, and this time she and the chair almost tipped over.

"So you have the answer now?"

"Yes," she lied, tired of being pushed around. It was time to push back. An explosion ripped through the quiet day and her jailer turned to gape. It was the opening she needed.

She used her manacled fists like a sledgehammer and caught him squarely in the jaw. He staggered and she spun, executing a perfect kick to his head, which sent him down to the ground. When he groaned and started to rise, she kicked him again.

Immediately, she bent down and searched him for the cuff keys. It took a second to get them off. She put them on him, hands behind his back, and then grabbed his gun.

She headed for the door, but when she was two feet from it, it burst open and men in black stood on the other side.

"Max!" she cried and ran to him as he took her into his arms and squeezed her tight, placing a kiss at her temple. That just wouldn't do. She grabbed the back of his head and pulled him down. She kissed him hard, his mouth as soft and clever as she remembered, the movement of his lips and tongue primal and greedy. She drew back and she stared up at him, a feline smile on her lips.

"Way to go, marine." Jason looked around. "Ha, superwoman took care of the guard. Didn't leave anything for us," he complained.

"We still have to get out of here," Max said, his words a rumble in his chest.

"How the hell did you find me?"

"A little birdie told us," replied Drew.

"I'll explain it to you later," Max said. "Let's get out of here before the whole compound realizes that explosion was just a diversionary tactic."

She nodded and Drew, Jason and Max led her out of the building into the jungle. Rio groaned to herself...not the jungle again.

"Don't worry, this time we've got a ride," Max murmured as they flanked her. But men came running from the side and they had to detour away from the vehicle.

"Mendez, get out of here and meet us at the rendezvous point. Ten minutes!" Drew said into his ear mic.

Max backed her up against a tree trunk, shielding her body with his. "This isn't working out like we planned." He leaned out and fired, then instantly ducked back as shots came. "Okay, going this way is not an option." He flashed her a smile. "Miller, we're going to have to go around."

Drew nodded and pointed to a copse of trees. Jason gave a quick nod of his head and melted into the underbrush.

"That way," Drew said, pointing.

She ran and found they had cover from Jason in the underbrush. Max stayed between her and the flying bullets. But whenever she could get a round off, she didn't hesitate.

"Go, go!" Drew yelled.

Rio ran full out, her aching body somehow coming up with the speed she needed. She was thankful for the adrenaline.

The Jeep, with Leila Mendez behind the wheel, skidded to a stop on the road. They all scrambled into the vehicle. Jason materialized out of the trees to jump in at the last minute.

"Gun it," Drew yelled. Leila stomped the gas and the Jeep jerked ahead, gaining speed.

Drew said into his ear mic, "Base, we've got Mary. Time to go. We're coming in hot."

"Mary?" Rio asked.

"Poppins," Max responded with a smile. "You needed a code name."

"You're going to pay for that later."

"I'll look forward to it," he said.

"Leila, up ahead," Drew noted.

"I see him, Captain," she replied, her voice as calm as if she was taking a Sunday drive. But she kept the course.

Rio jerked her eyes forward to see a black SUV heading right for them, and the crazy woman behind the wheel wasn't swerving.

"Leila…" Drew said, warning in his voice. "What have I told you about playing chicken?"

"I got it covered," Leila assured him. At the very last minute, she swerved and went off the road. The Jeep skidded, but the four-wheel drive saved them. Back on the road, Leila let out a shout of laughter.

When they hit the airport gates, Leila cruised through without stopping. The black SUV was right behind them. She drove right up to the plane and everyone scrambled out.

"Gotta love those Watchdog contacts," Drew said, grinning at Max. "Move, people," Drew shouted as they all hotfooted it to the jet.

Rio could hear the jet engines firing up as the black SUV screamed onto the runway and let loose with automatic gunfire.

"Buckle in," Leila yelled as she slammed into the cockpit and dropped into the copilot's chair. "I think my visit home has been productive. Let's get the hell out of Dodge, Frost."

Frost increased engine speed and the plane started to move as Rio buckled herself into one of the cushy seats. Max settled in beside her and Drew and Jason behind them.

The plane accelerated fast as Frost did some quick talking to the tower. After a tense moment, the tower cleared them and the silver jet shot into the air, leaving the pursuing SUV in its wake.

Frost banked the plane and Rio could see the men below them grow smaller and smaller by the minute. She turned to Max and kissed him again. "Thank you for coming for me."

"Hey, what about us?" Jason reminded her.

Rio got up and kissed him on the cheek. "Thank you one and all. I'm very lucky that my bodyguard is so well connected."

"I brought you clean clothes," Max said. "Need help changing?"

She smiled and rose, grabbing the bag. "I think I can manage."

"I can take care of the worst of those cuts and scratches," Jason offered. "After you've had a shower."

Rio's eyes lit up. "A shower," she said with reverence. Rio couldn't take her eyes off Max, who looked so commando in his black body armor and his ear mic.

"That look suits you, Marine."

"Are you sure you don't need help?"

"Well, I am pretty sore," she acknowledged, with a sly wink.

Max rose and followed her to the shower. Before she removed a stitch of clothing, she wrapped her arms around him and held on.

Max said, "I think we have a lot to talk about, Rio."

"Yes, but not now."

Her heart skipped a beat. The reckoning was almost at hand. Her brain scrambled to weigh all the pros and cons, but it was in constant flux with the reactions of her body and her heart. Both were in such a huge jumble, there was no way she could make any rational judgments. Not with him looking at her like that, and her wanting all sorts of things that were in direct conflict with one another.

The fallout she could expect from her boss was minor compared with what she wanted to tell Max, do to Max. She was afraid she might have ruined everything with her lies, deceit and her inability to get over her fear.

"No, not now," he said, his eyes filled with compassion and something she was afraid was everything she wanted. Was she strong enough, smart enough, to finally reach out and grasp it?

Right now, her pressing need was to be clean and to have Max hold her. Just hold her.

"Shower," he said softly, and he started helping her out of her clothes.

But her mind wouldn't stop spinning, teasing her with ridiculous possibilities, ones that should certainly seem outrageous at best, terrifying at worst. And yet she couldn't stop that tiny voice from whispering, tauntingly, teasingly, that perhaps it was possible they could be together. And he'd be the one man with whom maybe, just maybe, she could have it all.

He was so reverent as he removed everything from her aching body. "Let me do this for you, Rio," he asked, never more sincere, real concern outlined in every inch of his handsome face.

This time her heart didn't skip; it thundered with anticipation. In that moment, she knew she loved Max more than she'd ever loved a man before or ever would.

The risk of losing her heart was over. She'd already lost it to Max. There was no going back.

But was she going to move forward? She was so exhausted, just the act of lifting her leg out of her filthy shorts was an effort.

He turned on the water and gathered towels, liquid soap and a washcloth while the water heated. Then he stripped down to his bare skin, the black body armor revealing the hard, thick-muscled man beneath.

He helped her into the shower and she sighed as the heated water hit her skin. Clutching the handrail for support, she leaned back against Max. He soaped the cloth and dragged it over her shoulders, down the slopes of her breasts and stomach, over her legs, gently picking up each foot and massaging it clean while she braced herself on his powerful shoulder.

As the dirt washed away, so did all her barriers against this man and his gentle loving.

When they were finished, she tucked her head on his shoulder and blew out a long, shaky breath. "Thank you." She smiled against his warm, slippery skin.

Max tipped her chin up and kissed her...a slow, tender kiss. The kind that made her want to curl up with him and fall asleep in his arms.

"Did I mention this plane has a bed?"

"You must have read my mind."

"I was thinking of sleeping."

"No, you weren't, but that's okay. I love that you're trying to take care of me."

He smiled and with one of the white fluffy towels dried her off. Then he helped her into the underwear, soft cotton shorts and roomy T-shirt he brought for her. "I have street clothes in here for you when we land. But I thought you'd want to sleep until we get to L.A."

"You're so thoughtful. Where's the bed?"

"First aid first."

Max dressed in similar clothing. With her hair up in one of the other towels, he led her from the steamy bathroom back to Jason, who took care of her cuts.

Frost left the pilot's chair and Drew took his place.

"Max, I found your mole."

"You already got through all the DEA and FBI security?"

"Nah, didn't have to. I hacked in to Fuentes's records

and traced the money. He had some pretty serious fire-walls, but they're no match for me. I wrote the name down for you and as soon as we get to a place where I can print, I'll give you the evidence I have."

"Thanks, Frost. That's a relief," Rio said. "Where was the mole? In the DEA or FBI?"

"DEA, love. Sorry."

A few minutes later Max led her down the passage-way to an accordion door. Opening it, they went inside.

Rio took one look at the bed and headed right for it. She unwound the towel and quickly combed her hair, braiding it loosely. Max pulled down the comforter and sheets and they both slipped inside.

He pulled her into his arms just as she snuggled against him. "I was so scared that I'd be too late," he whispered against her damp hair.

"But you weren't, Max. You saved me." In more ways than one, she thought.

"I had help."

"That little birdie you told me about? Who?"

"The Ghost."

She stiffened and stared at Max, pleading with him for the answer she needed.

"I asked him point-blank if he was Shane McMas-ters."

"His answer?"

"Rio, he said Shane no longer existed."

She closed her eyes and settled into Max's warmth. "Is that right?" And still, that was no answer at all.

As she drifted off to sleep, she couldn't be sure, but she thought she heard Max say, "I love you."

13

THE FOLLOWING DAY, dressed in a blue pencil skirt and a white blouse, Rio found herself back in that conference room where she'd first met Max.

He was standing next to her, impeccable in a dark blue suit, starched white shirt and red tie, the quintessential FBI agent.

They had made their report to both her boss and his, Michael Drake. They left nothing out except the exact Watchdog personnel who'd helped them and the personal stuff. She didn't think either one of them wanted to hear about her and Max having sex.

But, of course, it was so much more than that.

The mole, a veteran agent who had expected to retire off what he had made with Fuentes's blood money, had been arrested. He was now going to spend the rest of his life behind bars. If he lasted. Even inmates didn't like a squealer.

There was only one terrible nagging question she had yet to ask the DEA director, Russell Sanford, and her "talk" with Max was still hanging over her.

Sanford said, "Neither Michael nor I can fault you for carrying out your duty, but we should have been con-

sulted. It was resourceful of you to launch the rescue of
my agent, Mr. Carpenter. But you both could have dis-
rupted a very important undercover operation an agent
has given so much for."

Rio cleared her throat. "Would that agent be my
brother, Shane McMasters?"

Her boss gave absolutely nothing away as he stared
at her. Rio didn't move or blink. She faced him squarely.
She *had* to know.

Sanford's features gentled. "Your brother died a hero
in the line of duty, Agent Marshall. He has nothing to
do with this operation."

"I find that interesting, Director, as the man I saw in
Fuentes's compound looked very much like my
brother."

"I assure you. Your brother is dead, Rio. Let it go."

It was almost an order.

"Did you assign me to Agent Carpenter to keep us
both busy?" she persisted. "He was obsessed with the
Ghost, and I, which is now obvious to me, saw something I shouldn't have."

The director pinned her with an irritated glare.
"Shane is gone and we can't bring him back. I know that
must be painful for you. I will overlook your questions."

"So we're done here?" Max asked.

"Not quite," Sanford said. "For your continued
safety, we are going to be sending you to an undis-
closed safe place until this operation is complete."

"Not another island," Rio groaned.

"I'm not going to reveal that information. In fact,

I've handed this over to the very capable hands of people I trust."

"Yes, sir," Rio said.

They were escorted out of the DEA headquarters to a waiting car.

Once inside Rio turned to Max. "Feels like déjà vu, huh?"

"Yeah, but there's a big difference here."

"What's that?"

"There's no hidden agenda."

"I wouldn't say that," she said. It was time for her to lay her heart on the line.

"What do you mean?"

"Not now. Wait until we get somewhere more private."

He nodded.

They were taken back to LAX and another waiting jet. Once aboard, Max relaxed when he found Drew behind the controls and Jason riding as copilot.

"Looks like you both weathered the storm," Drew said.

"I think it helped that we knew who the mole was and could back it up with evidence. Thanks to you and your team, Drew."

"You're welcome, Marine. Strap in and let's get you to your destination."

"And that's where?" Max asked.

"Need-to-know basis, my friend. Sorry."

Max chuckled as he sat down next to Rio.

The plane took off and Max got up and looked in the fridge. "Hey, there's champagne in here."

"Open it up, Max. We have something to celebrate."

Max did the honors and soon had two sparkling glasses for them to sip from. Before she took her glass, she pulled the privacy curtain.

"Sit down, Max." She took her glass from him and sat down in a chair facing him.

"I want to explain something to you and it's going to be difficult enough to say, so please try not to interrupt me until I'm finished."

"Okay," he said, his expression serious and intent.

"When I lost my parents, it was devastating to me. Then, a year later, I lost Shane. I had no one left. My family was gone. That makes a person sorta shrink into herself.

"I decided to join the DEA because I thought I could make a difference and, yes, I also thought I could nail Fuentes. It was one of my major goals.

"After mourning my family, I shut down emotionally. I vowed I wouldn't get involved again because I couldn't bear to love and lose someone."

She took comfort from the hand Max placed on her arm and the slow caress.

"Then I came along?"

"Yes," she said, her voice going teary. "I tried to fight it and think this would all end and we'd go our separate ways."

"I don't want to go our separate ways."

She didn't argue. He made a good point. He usually did. She'd like to believe she'd be thinking more clearly if he wasn't around, but the fact was, they did make a good team. They both had sharp minds and strong instincts. And they were so very good in bed.

"That's good," she said, tears spilling down her cheeks, "because I love you, Max."

In the next instant, she found herself spun directly into his arms and being very soundly kissed. By the time she got her senses back, he was already lifting his head.

"I love you, too, Rio. I know we can make this work."

"Let's drink to that." She reached for the two flutes. They clinked their glasses together then drained them. "If one sip is good luck, then the whole glass should make us the luckiest couple on the planet."

He released her then hauled her right back in and kissed her again, only this time he lingered before lifting his head. Her heart tightened in her chest at the depth of her feeling for this man.

"Can I talk now?"

"Yes, you can."

"I had my own problems, you know. You were right, I have…had control issues. As the eldest child in the family, it came naturally to me. But being together is about trust and you have mine, and I already know I have yours. So we both learned something on this journey."

She nodded. "I love you, Max, so much."

"I don't think I'll ever get tired of hearing that."

"What do you want to do while we're getting to this unknown destination?"

He just grinned.

Okay, he also made her think about that. A lot. And she remembered Max peeling himself out of that black body armor. "You are a bad boy, Special Agent Max Carpenter."

"I didn't say a word."

"You didn't have to."

They both laughed as they made their way back to the bedroom, not caring where they were going as long as they were going together.

* * * * *

THE RANGER & HOT-BLOODED
(2-IN-1 ANTHOLOGY)

BY RHONDA NELSON & KAREN FOLEY

The Ranger

Will Forrester—former Army Ranger—has his work cut out for him. Rhiannon Palmer's the most stubborn, flat-out sexy woman he's ever encountered. And he can't keep his hands off her.

Hot-Blooded

First Sergeant Chase McCormick isn't a chauvinist. But he does believe that women have no place in combat zones. Why? Because his men forget their training! He wouldn't do that!

3 SEDUCTIONS AND A WEDDING
BY JULIE LETO

Jessie might not forgive Leo for his long-ago betrayal, but after one scorching kiss, she can't fight the chemistry any more. But a girl can't base her future on great sex. Or can she?

MY FAKE FIANCÉE
BY NANCY WARREN

Chelsea Hammond will live with David Wolfe temporarily in order for him to clinch a massive promotion. Newly returned from Paris, she'll use his kitchen for her new catering business. *Strictly business...*

**On sale from 20th May 2011
Don't miss out!**

Available at WHSmith, Tesco, ASDA, Eason and all good bookshops

www.millsandboon.co.uk

0511/14

MILLS & BOON®

are proud to present our...

Book of the Month

Come to Me
by Linda Winstead Jones

from Mills & Boon® Intrigue

Lizzie needs PI Sam's help in looking for her lost
half-sister. Sam's always had a crush on Lizzie.
But moving in on his former partner's daughter
would be *oh-so-wrong*…

Available 15th April

Something to say about our Book of the Month?
Tell us what you think!

millsandboon.co.uk/community
facebook.com/romancehq
twitter.com/millsandboonuk

BAD BLOOD

A POWERFUL
DYNASTY,
WHERE SECRETS
AND SCANDAL
NEVER SLEEP!

VOLUME 1 – 15th April 2011
TORTURED RAKE
by Sarah Morgan

VOLUME 2 – 6th May 2011
SHAMELESS PLAYBOY
by Caitlin Crews

VOLUME 3 – 20th May 2011
RESTLESS BILLIONAIRE
by Abby Green

VOLUME 4 – 3rd June 2011
FEARLESS MAVERICK
by Robyn Grady

8 VOLUMES IN ALL TO COLLECT!

www.millsandboon.co.uk

Intense passion and glamour from our bestselling stars of international romance

Available 20th May 2011

Available 17th June 2011

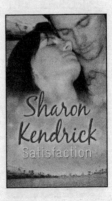

Available 15th July 2011

Available 19th August 2011

One night with a hot-blooded male!

One night in MILAN

MICHELLE REID · INDIA GREY · KATE HEWITT

18th February 2011

One night in RIO

ANNE MATHER · JENNIE LUCAS · OLIVIA GATES

18th March 2011

One night in BUENOS AIRES

MAGGIE COX · CHANTELLE SHAW · SARAH MORGAN

15th April 2011

One night in MADRID

KATE WALKER · JENNIE LUCAS · ABBY GREEN

20th May 2011

MILLS & BOON

www.millsandboon.co.uk

Meet the three Keyes sisters—in Susan Mallery's unmissable family saga

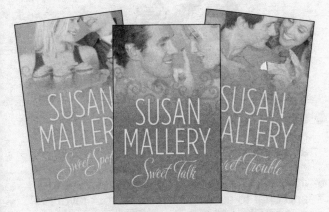

Sweet Talk
Available 18th March 2011

Sweet Spot
Available 15th April 2011

Sweet Trouble
Available 20th May 2011

For "readers who can't get enough of Nora Roberts' family series"—Booklist

www.millsandboon.co.uk

2 FREE BOOKS
AND A SURPRISE GIFT

We would like to take this opportunity to thank you for reading this Mills & Boon® book by offering you the chance to take TWO more specially selected titles from the Blaze® series absolutely FREE! We're also making this offer to introduce you to the benefits of the Mills & Boon® Book Club™—

- **FREE home delivery**
- **FREE gifts and competitions**
- **FREE monthly Newsletter**
- **Exclusive Mills & Boon Book Club offers**
- **Books available before they're in the shops**

Accepting these FREE books and gift places you under no obligation to buy, you may cancel at any time, even after receiving your free books. Simply complete your details below and return the entire page to the address below. You don't even need a stamp!

YES Please send me 2 free Blaze books and a surprise gift. I understand that unless you hear from me, I will receive 3 superb new books every month, including a 2-in-1 book priced at £5.30 and two single books priced at £3.30 each, postage and packing free. I am under no obligation to purchase any books and may cancel my subscription at any time. The free books and gift will be mine to keep in any case.

Ms/Mrs/Miss/Mr_____ Initials _____

_____

Surname _____

Address _____

_____

_____ Postcode _____

E-mail _____

Send this whole page to: Mills & Boon Book Club, Free Book Offer, FREEPOST NAT 10298, Richmond, TW9 1BR